Deadly Vintage

To Renee Grandinetti - Enjoy the mystery — and enjoy Portugal! *Elizabeth Varadan*

Deadly Vintage

By

Elizabeth Varadan

Belanger Books
2019

Deadly Vintage

ISBN: 9781712268469

For information contact:
Belanger Books, LLC
61 Theresa Ct.
Manchester, NH 03103
derrick@belangerbooks.com
www.belangerbooks.com

Cover and Back design by Brian Belanger
www.belangerbooks.com and
www.redbubble.com/people/zhahadun

Dedication

This book is for my husband, Rajan

Table of Contents

Chapter One - A Fine Bottle of Port 11

Chapter Two - Polícia!...............24

Chapter Three - Only a Statement, Nothing More........33

Chapter Four – Something Weird Was Going On 38

Chapter Five – What Harm Can a Little Investigating Do? 42

Chapter Six – In the Jardim de Santa Bárbara............52

Chapter Seven - A Visit to Paulo 66

Chapter Eight - Detective Fernandes Comes Calling 72

Chapter Nine - Carla Pays a Visit of Her Own 82

Chapter Ten - A Sharper Focus...............92

Chapter Eleven – A Threatening Message 99

Chapter Twelve - Carla Tells All and Learns a Few Things 104

Chapter Thirteen - A Rude Surprise 109

Chapter Fourteen – A Change in Plans 116

Chapter Fifteen - Some Disconcerting News...............126

Chapter Sixteen - A New Friend...............135

Chapter Seventeen – An Expedition 145

Chapter Eighteen – Dinner at A Taberna do Félix 158

Chapter Nineteen - Going, Going, Gone 164

Chapter Twenty – A Jarring Conversation...............174

Chapter Twenty-One – Candy Wrappers and Doldrums 178

Chapter Twenty-Two - Shoes, Beautiful Shoes 181

Chapter Twenty-Three - Coffee with a Culprit...........187

Chapter Twenty-Four – Realizations.........................197

Chapter Twenty-Five – Can We Talk? 210

Chapter Twenty-Six –Because of Family 222

Chapter Twenty-Seven – The Best Laid Plans 231

Chapter Twenty-Eight – All's Well That Ends Well—for Some...240

Chapter Twenty-Nine – A Fine Alvarinho 245

Acknowledgements 249

About the Author...251

Chapter One - A Fine Bottle of Port

Carla Bass paused at the corner souvenir shop, a pie-wedge shaped building. She was returning from an antique store where she'd seen a gilt-framed mirror one of her clients might like. The narrow street to the right had intrigued her for some time. Linden trees unfurled dark green, heart-shaped leaves on the shop side of the cobbled street. Across from the shop, a salmon-colored door and awning of a small café matched two open umbrellas at outside tables. Above the door and plate glass window, pots of red geraniums lined the balcony.

Perfect for a new blog post. Already words were coming to her: "Capture the eye-catching charm of Portugal on your own back patio . . .", *or some such.* A sliding glass door could substitute for the plate glass window. At first Carla had worried about how to conduct her interior design business from abroad, but her blog and Skype meetings with her partner, Bethany, made it surprisingly easy.

During the six weeks Carla Bass and her husband had been in Braga, Portugal had felt like a grand adventure. While Owen oversaw a hotel remodel for his employer's new chain, her interior design business was enjoying a boost. She had started a blog, posting snapshots of tiled walls and wrought iron balconies. She'd bought a Portuguese grammar book and another fat volume, *621 Portuguese Verbs*, given that the remodel was expected to take six months.

The cool breeze stirring the air felt fresh on her face. Late April mornings were still crisp in Braga. In fact, the weather reminded her of Piedmont, California, where her and Owen's friends were taking turns house-sitting.

She took her small Lumix camera out of her handbag and walked past the souvenir shop to get a good shot of the café. The wine shop next door caught her attention instead. The set of tiles across the front was different from the traditional azulejo tiles decorating facades and entrances of so many buildings: It showed a wine harvest scene above the doorway. Blue and white depictions of grape clusters framed the plate window and each side of the door. Owen might like a pictorial effect like this for the hotel. Only last night he'd said his team was considering azulejos for the facade.

The hotel also planned to offer more than one Port. This shop probably had a good selection. She took out her phone from her handbag and dialed her husband.

"Hi, babe," he answered. She pictured his lopsided smile, the dimples that always made him look boyish, despite the way his blonde hair was starting to thin above his temples.

"I'm at a wine shop with an incredible doorway you should see." she said. "I'm taking pictures. Do you want to meet me at Centésima Página for a quick lunch and have a look? You might get some ideas for your entrance." Centésima Página was a combined bookstore and eatery on Avenida Central, a few hundred yards from the hotel remodel he was overseeing.

"I've got a meeting at two," he said. "Twelve-thirty okay?"

"Twelve-thirty it is." They exchanged their usual phone kisses and Carla hung up.

Picking her way across cobbled street in her stiletto heels, she walked to the front of the café and turned to view the wine shop. A tall, weathered wooden gate separated it from the corner shop on the left. To the right, a lacey wrought-iron balcony above an ochre wall set off the blue of the tiles.

Just as she raised her camera, a gaunt-faced man exited the shop. He wore a dark suit, old fashioned in a way she couldn't put her finger on, and he walked past the souvenir shop and around the corner with a surprisingly energetic step for his age. His high forehead and flattened gray hair made her think of old Boris Karloff movies on the TV classics station at home.

She raised her camera again, then lowered it, annoyed as another man came from the other direction and paused by the door, blocking a few tiles on the doorway's frame. With an air that struck her as almost furtive, he glanced around before stepping inside.

Carla had seen him before, but where? Sharp profile, white goatee, hair stylishly fringing the collar of his shirt. Designer jeans. Even the swagger was familiar. While she was framing a horizontal shot of the doorway, it came to her: Last week he was at a viewing for the upcoming estate auction this Thursday evening. They hadn't exchanged two words, but she'd caught him checking her out. Ogling was more like it. *Too young for you, buddy,* she'd thought.

She took a second, vertical shot and was tucking the camera back into its cloth case when he came out again, his jaw set in a determined line. This time he looked briefly in her direction, but he seemed so preoccupied she doubted he recognized her. He strode down the street the way he had come, practically slamming his feet against the walk, his hands curling and flexing, as if he wanted to punch someone.

Nice guy—not!

Carla crossed over and entered the shop. A bell tinkled above her head. Shelves filled with bottles of regular wines and Ports met her eyes. A glass case in the wall on her right housed a bottle that seemed on special display. In a corner alcove, a table and two chairs were set up for tasting.

To her left, the proprietor in a black vest and white shirtsleeves gave Carla an appraising glance. Gray flecked his temples and his thick mustache. "Bom dia," he said.

"Bom dia." Carla matched his pronunciation, making it sound like "bong dia." Despite her best efforts, trying to pronounce Portuguese was making her crazy. Portuguese was filled with nasalized vowels and consonants whose rules seemed to shift from gutturals to whispers. Still, even though most of the locals in shops and restaurants knew English, Carla found them especially friendly if she tried to speak Portuguese. She took out the small dictionary tucked in her purse and looked up "bottle."

"Por favor, queria . . . uma garrafa . . . do Porto."

"I speak a little English, senhora," the proprietor said, drawing out "little" to "leetle." With a quick glance at something below the counter, he asked, "What kind of Port you want? You are in the land of great Port. We invent it, you know."

Carla put her dictionary back in her handbag. "I would actually like your advice."

"Ah. Senhor Costa at your service. I am pleased to advise such pretty lady." He inclined his head in a way that suggested a bow, and came around the counter, hands clasped behind his back. "You are inglesa? English?"

"Americana," Carla said. "My husband is coordinating the remodel of a new hotel branch of World Portal Inns." Senhor Costa tilted his head, as if trying to remember the name. "A boutique hotel, part of a California chain—on Avenida Central. On Praça República," she added.

Senhor Costa nodded. "Sim. Yes, I know it. Not far from here, near the Arcada and the fountain."

"That's the one."

"That already used to be a nice hotel."

"It will be again," she assured him. "The grand opening isn't until September. He's planning to keep the building's character, with the restaurant and bar in front, and a gardened terrace with tables at the side."

"A nice feature. I remember."

"And he plans to offer a fine Port in the bar. More than one Port, probably." Actually, the bar manager, Tiago, would be making the selections, but he was open to suggestions.

"Ah! A fine Port for hotel bar. I think of three you like. Come." Senhor Costa led her to the corner alcove where the table and two small chairs nestled. Several glasses were clustered in the center of the table, along with a box of crackers, a dish, and a wine opener with a metal top shaped like a bunch of grapes.

"Please sit. I will bring some to taste." Senhor Costa walked over to the wall of shelves. Carla smoothed her pencil skirt and sat. The faint, fruity aroma of an earlier tasting hovered in the alcove. He selected three bottles, and set them before her, then uncorked one and poured a splash into a glass.

"You like one of these, the hotel will buy more from me, eh?" He winked and his smile widened, revealing a set of white, even teeth that would have made any Hollywood celebrity proud. He uncorked the second bottle, shook some crackers into the dish, and waited, hands clasped behind his back.

"Very nice," Carla said, after sipping the first sample, "but a little sweet."

He pursed his lips. "Is very good with Azeitão cheese."

Carla shook her head and nibbled one of the crackers. He poured a sample from the new bottle, and she took a sip of the shimmering red liquid. Fruity, as she expected. *Good, though.*

It was the tawny Port, deep orange in color, with its nutty taste and velvety texture that decided her. "This one!"

Senhor Costa looked pleased. "Suave, no? How do you say? Smooth. Ten years old." He quoted her the price and she felt her brows lift. But Owen's employer wanted the new branch of World Portal Inns to be upscale as well as comfortable and inviting. She took another sip, letting it linger on her tongue.

"I have twenty-year Port, too," Senhor Costa said. "Ver-ra smooth."

"I'll take a bottle of this for now," Carla said. "If my husband recommends it, we'll be back for more." Owen would probably be interested in the twenty-year Port as well. It was important to offer guests a range, and Tiago would appreciate that.

To her surprise, Senhor Costa half-filled her glass again and poured a half-glass for himself, holding it toward her to toast. "Saúde," he said.

"I haven't eaten yet," Carla protested.

Senhor Costa shrugged. "We drink to more bottles in the future. I know your husband will like this." His soft accent turned "this" into "theesh."

The phone rang while he took a new, unopened bottle to the counter, muttering, "I put this in bag for you." Carla idly brushed a few scattered cracker crumbs into a neat little pile at the corner of the table while he took the call.

"Olá," she heard; then, more sharply, "Não! Não o tenho!" Senhor Costa banged down the receiver.

Carla ran through the few Portuguese words she knew. "Tenho" meant, "I have." "Não" meant "no." *No! I don't have! Or maybe, No! I don't have* it!" When she peered around at him, Costa had propped his elbows on the counter and was massaging his forehead. His grimace suggested worry or pain.

"Do you have a headache?" Carla asked. "I have aspirin." She started rummaging through her purse.

"Pah! No headache. This crazy person keep calling to sell me bad wine I don't want." With a sweep of his arm, Senhor Costa told her, "Take a look around my shop." He attempted a grin. "Maybe you see some other wine for your hotel wine bar, eh? A good vinho verde, maybe."

Carla got up and browsed the shelves, more to let him regain his composure than to inspect wines or Ports. Her stiletto heels echoed on the hardwood floor. Her chest was warm from the Ports she had sampled. She felt a little light-headed. At the glass display case by the window, she scrutinized the curious-shaped bottle inside. The long neck topped a bell-shaped body that bore the label, "Manoel Beleza de Andrade, 1812." A hand-printed sign next to it read, "€3.000,00."

"Have you had many offers?" Carla asked.

17

She turned and found Senhor Costa watching her, a thoughtful expression on his face as he twisted the top of the wine bottle bag.

"There are those who will pay much more for the right bottle, senhora. Eighteen-twelve was historic time for Portugal. For France, also. Manoel Beleza de Andrade was one of Douro region's leading vintners. But, no, senhora. No one has shown interest in this one."

"It must be like drinking money—a hundred euros a sip," Carla said, attempting a joke.

The proprietor shrugged. "The Port is not always to drink. Very rich people like to show on."

"Show off," she corrected, then worried she might have hurt his feelings, but he only nodded abstractedly.

A crazy way to show off. Why buy a Port you don't plan to drink? Briefly Carla wondered if Mrs. Demming, her client in Belvedere, would love showing off such a bottle. No. Mrs. Demming, was into 19th century furniture, Old World paintings, statues, vases, mirrors, clocks. She'd been delighted when Carla told her she would be going to Portuguese auctions and antique shops. Which reminded Carla to tell Bethany about the gilt-framed mirror during their Skype meeting this evening.

Senhor Costa's voice broke into her thoughts. "Maybe you will take a picture to show your husband what crazy people will buy."

"Oh, he'd love that!" Carla chuckled and set her glass on a shelf next to the glass case. She took her camera from her handbag again and snapped two close-ups of the odd-looking bottle. Then she walked over and paid Senhor Costa for the Port, carefully counting out the correct euros.

"Obrigado," he said, thanking her, and handed her the bag.

"Obrigado," she echoed.

"Obrigada," he corrected.

She sighed, momentarily defeated. *The gender thing.* "I keep forgetting."

To get back to what she hoped was a graceful exit, she said, "I appreciate the samples. You have a lovely shop."

He nodded. "I will see you again."

To buy more Port? That's confidence! She smiled at him. "You could be right."

Braga was a large city, spreading into the surrounding mountains and forests and climbing up hillsides. A few tall, modern buildings were interspersed with older stone architecture. The historic center where she and Owen had an apartment was like a small village set inside the city. Nearly everything was in walking distance: the hotel whose remodel Owen was overseeing, antique shops, restaurants, cafés, an abundance of churches, museums. Even the house with the estate auction Thursday night, where Carla would be bidding on two paintings by Da Silva Porto. As she left the wine shop, bells from Igreja dos Congregados started tolling the noon hour, echoed by the bells of Sé Catedral. She had thirty minutes to drop off the Port at the apartment and walk back up to the bookstore café to meet Owen.

Hurrying down Rua dos Chãos, she rounded the corner of the Baroque Banco de Portugal, just two doors from the new hotel. Scaffolding and netting covered the hotel's front. For a moment, Carla was tempted to sneak under the netting and go inside to show Owen the Port. But it would be more fun to surprise him this evening after the Portuguese meal she planned. She crossed the Praça da República and hurried along Avenida Central past the Igreja de Nossa Senhora a Branca (the Church of Our Lady in White) on her left. Their corner apartment was across the street beyond.

She entered the vestibule with its opposite French door overlooking the back garden. The entrance to a second, ground-floor apartment was next to the stairs, but she'd never seen the tenant. She climbed to their first -floor apartment, since there was no elevator. Once inside, she set her purse down and took the wine bag to the kitchen, putting it on the granite counter.

When she pulled out the bottle, she nearly dropped it. The faded label showed it was an 1863 Vintage Port from Quinto do Vezuvio. At the bottom edge, a signature scrawled in ink that once must have been dark but now had faded to a pale rust, said, "Obrigado, Duque . . ." followed by a dramatically curly C and J, and then ". . . de Acaer."

"Duque" had to be Duke. From someplace called Acaer. C for Carlos? Cesar? J for José? Juan? A bottle signed by a duke must be worth thousands of dollars!

I have to call Senhor Costa. She couldn't. She didn't have his number. Or his first name. She didn't even have the name of the shop. She had to take it back to him. She set the bottle on the entry table, pulled her mobile phone out of her handbag, and dialed Owen's number.

"Hi, babe. What's up?" he asked.

"I'll be a few minutes late," Carla said. "I have to return a bottle of Port to the wine shop I told you about."

"Take it after lunch," Owen said amiably. "What's the rush?"

"I'll explain when I see you." Carla hung up and started to put the bottle back in the bag, then hesitated. This

20

was the closest she would ever come to having a nineteenth-century bottle of Port in her possession.

Make that an 1863 Vintage Port autographed by a duke. She quickly snapped two pictures of the label on her Lumix, stuffed the camera back into her purse, grabbed the bottle by the neck, and dashed out.

When she reached the shop, walking as quickly as her stiletto heels would let her, she stopped to catch her breath. Church bells pealed again—twelve-thirty. Some shops closed for an hour-and-a-half lunch period, but the sign on the wine shop door still said "Aberto." She went in.

Senhor Costa wasn't at the counter, and the tinkling bell didn't bring him. The shop was empty. Grasping the bottle, Carla looked around, then froze when she saw the shattered display case. Shards of glass were scattered across the floor, along with small gleaming splinters that shimmered in the light from the street window. The 1812 Manoel Beleza de Andrade Port was gone. *Stolen.* That much was clear. She was acutely aware of the duke's bottle she was clutching. A bottle that might be as expensive, if not more. Her mouth felt suddenly dry. What if the thief were still here?

Get a grip! Would he hang around once he had what he came for?

Beyond the end of the counter, a door she hadn't noticed earlier was wide open.

"Senhor Costa?" she called softly. There was no answer.

She walked over and entered, cautiously scanning the room. Obviously, his office. Magazines were neatly stacked at one corner of a boxy desk to the right. In the center of the desk was a black laptop computer. At one side, a folder stuffed with papers lay next to a stack of envelopes. A scrap of gold shiny paper on the floor caught her eye, a candy wrapper that had missed the wastebasket next to the swivel chair. Senhor Costa must have a sweet tooth. Absently, Carla picked the wrapper up, crinkled it into a small ball, and tossed it in the wastebasket. Across from the desk was a side door, and a window next to it looked out on an outdoor corridor between Senhor Costa's shop and the corner souvenir shop. That explained the wooden gate she'd noticed earlier. She peeped out the window, but there was no sign of Costa. On the other side of the patio-like space, a door that must be to the souvenir shop was closed.

Pursing her lips, she looked back at the desk. Behind it, another door, ajar, opened on stairs that must go down to a wine cellar. For a moment, Carla considered going to the top of the stairs and calling, then hesitated. Senhor Costa *could* be downstairs, checking on his inventory. Say he had been in the bathroom, wherever that was, when the burglary had happened, and now he wanted to see what else had been taken.

But what if the thief was downstairs, looking for other rare ports? She looked at the bottle in her hand.

Like, say, an 1863 Vintage Port from Quinto do Vezuvio. Autographed by a duke.

She'd be smart to leave the duke's bottle on the counter with a note to Senhor Costa.

She came through the door to the shop, wondering what to write. The emptiness of the room made her skin prickle as she walked to the counter. Did Costa go for help while the thief was smashing up his display counter? Something didn't feel right. Setting the bottle on the counter, she fished in her purse for the little notebook she always carried. She leaned forward to write her note. And then she saw it—the proprietor's crumpled figure behind the counter. He was sprawled on his back, his hands splayed against the floor, as though he had staggered backwards, then tried to break his fall. His eyes stared glassily at the ceiling. An angry, bruised lump swelled above his forehead over his left eyebrow. Something shiny and white protruded from the corner of his mouth. With a start, Carla realized it was his dentures and fought a giddy urge to laugh, as if that might hold off the deeper realization seeping into her mind with numbing chill.

Senhor Costa was quite dead.

Chapter Two - Polícia!

Carla held the bottle against her chest to calm her trembling. She needed to call the police. She could kick herself for not following the advice in *Living in Portugal* to enter emergency numbers in her mobile phone. Still, what were her chances of being understood over the phone? She should find someone to make the call for her.

Outside, she looked around. Across the street, a dark-haired man whose scruffy jeans hung low on his narrow hips leaned carelessly against the wall beside the café. One hand held a pale sweatshirt draped over his shoulder. A cigarette dangled from his lip. He watched her with interest. Curiosity, Carla supposed uneasily, but something about him was off-putting. Maybe she should go to the corner souvenir shop next door instead and ask for help. At least she knew the words for that: "Ajudem-me!"

The man straightened, tossed his cigarette to the pavement, and crossed the street, the sweatshirt in his hand. "Why you are upset, senhora?" he asked.

Relief that he spoke English mingled with suspicion. There was a jackal-like quality to his posture, as if waiting. A faint scar on his upper lip and another in the middle of his left eyebrow must have come from fights. He ran a hand over his dark, slicked-back hair.

"Maybe I help you." He eyed the bottle in her hand.

Despite her misgivings, Carla said, "Call the police. It's urgent."

24

"Why you want police?" he asked in a soothing tone that was almost hypnotic.

"A man is dead!"

"Dead?" He stepped closer. Instinctively she stepped back. "Where?" he asked.

"Inside. There's been a burglary, too. The thief might still be in there." Carla shuddered, remembering the wine-seller's sightless stare and the way his dentures jutted at such an odd angle.

"Maybe you are thief, eh?" The man nodded at the bottle she was holding.

Carla squared her shoulders. "I was trying to return *this!* He gave me it to me by mis—"

Before she could finish, he'd snatched the bottle out of her hands and took off running down the street, the soles of his trainers flashing. He nearly bumped into an old man who turned and shouted something, shaking his walking stick.

"Stop! Thief!" Carla screamed the only emergency word she could remember, "Ladrão," hoping she pronounced it right.

The thief dashed across the street and kept running past linden trees, past the pharmacy in the next street with its overhead green-cross logo, and disappeared around a far corner. She had an urge to run after him, but the thought of her stiletto heels and Senhor Costa lying on the floor brought her to her senses. She flagged the old man with the walking stick as he approached. He paused, politely, and adjusted the flat cap on his head, as she fumbled in her purse for her dictionary.

"Por favor . . . I mean . . . faz favor . . ." Seeing the map of wrinkles on his face, she wondered if such an old man would even have a cell phone. But he might at least know the number and be able to call on hers.

A young woman appeared at her elbow. A student, maybe. She wore jeans and had a book bag slung over her shoulder.

"Senhora, I saw that man steal your bottle. I speak English. I will call the police for you." She took a cell phone from her bag and tapped in the number. In a moment, she said, "Olá," and began speaking rapidly in Portuguese.

"Tell them a man inside the shop has been killed," Carla said. "The owner."

The young woman's face went ashen. "A man is killed?" At Carla's nod, she burst into a flood of Portuguese and Carla caught the words, "morto," then the address, and then, "Obrigada." When she hung up, she bowed her head, pressing the back of her hand against her forehead. In seconds, tears were streaming down her face.

"Did you know him?" Carla asked softly.

"He is my uncle."

"I'm so sorry." Carla looked away. "He was a nice man," she murmured, not knowing what else to say. His image flashed before her, hands behind his back, head cocked, while awaiting her verdict on the ruby Port.

The woman took out a handkerchief and dabbed her eyes and nose. "He was good to me," she said after a pause.

Pondering that, Carla called Owen, having to dial a second time because her fingers seemed to have become thumbs.

"Where are you?" he asked.

Suddenly the phone was shaking in Carla's hand. "I'm at the wine shop," she said, hearing the quaver in her voice. "I have to wait here for the police."

"The police!"

"A man's been killed. Can you come right away?" For the second time that day, she said, "I'll explain later." She gave him the address, adding, "It's the little cobbled street just off Rua dos Chãos. Just a street up from the bank and the hotel; it runs behind them, actually." The proximity gave her a sudden sense of calm. "There's a souvenir shop on the corner," she said. "The odd-shaped pie-wedge corner. The wine shop is right next door." She hung up to wait with Senhor Costa's niece, then introduced herself.

"Maria Santos," the niece said. Swiping her tears away, she added, "I must go see him," and started for the door.

"Whoever did it could still be in there," Carla warned, even though it was more likely she had just seen him run off with the duke's bottle. She told Maria about the other bottle stolen from the smashed case. "Did you see anyone go in and come out again?" she asked hopefully.

Maria averted her eyes. "I had just went for café across the street. I do that when I come for shopping. Then I come to say hello to my uncle. But I was reading a book. Then I saw you go in just now. Before that, I saw the man who stole your bottle go in and come out again. I thought he went away. He must have crossed the street only."

"He probably killed your uncle." Carla whispered. *And then stuck around to wait for the discovery. Like criminals do.* Or did in some of the mysteries she read. She fought the wave of nausea that was trying to well up from her stomach as she remembered his menacing face. *I came that close to a killer!*

A blue-and-white striped PSP car—Polícia de Segurança Pública— pulled up and parked. Two men in navy blue uniforms got out and approached Carla and Maria. Now that the police had arrived, the old man lingered at one side of the shop door, leaning on his walking stick, his face eager for gossip.

"Chefe de Polícia Esteves," the taller of the two introduced himself. A dark mustache draped across his upper lip like a furry caterpillar. Nodding toward his shorter, boxier companion, he added, "Agente Cunha." Agent Cunha hung his thumbs in his pockets and looked around, scanning the street in both directions. Across the street, in the café doorway, an older, rather dumpy woman stood watching.

"Who has found the body?" asked Chief Esteves. He repeated it in Portuguese.

"I did," Carla said. She explained how she had come back to return Senhor Costa's Port and found him dead. With a shudder, she said, "He's on the floor, behind the counter."

Maria stifled a sob.

"Show me," commanded Esteves, his hand on his Beretta as he accompanied the two women inside. Agent Cunha stayed outside to hold back onlookers who were starting to gather.

Chief Esteves looked at the glass on the floor from the broken case, rounded the end of the counter, and shook his head. He cautioned the women to stay where they were and went into the office. A moment later his steps sounded on the stairs to the cellar.

When he returned, he took a handkerchief from his pocket. Crouching beside Senhor Costa's inert form, he moved the dead man's head slightly to the right, revealing a wound with very little blood. "He hit his head behind. And then something has hit him hard on forehead." Looking up at Carla, he asked, "What time do you find him?"

"A few minutes ago, when I brought the bottle of Port back."

He rose, frowning. "And when were you here the first time?"

"It was a few minutes to twelve when I left."

"You are certain?"

"Yes. The church bells started ringing on my way home. Twelve times. I wanted to take the Port home before meeting my husband for lunch and thought I had just enough time."

"But it was the wrong bottle, you say."

"Yes."

"And a stranger stole it from you."

"Yes," Carla repeated nervously. No doubt he had to ask these questions, but did he have to sound so . . . suspicious?

"I saw the man steal her bottle," Maria assured him, then said something in Portuguese. At his next question, she inclined her head toward her dead uncle and said sadly, "Ele é meu tio."

Esteves's face softened, and he murmured what must be the equivalent of "I'm sorry."

To Carla, he said, "Do you know what was in that shelf?" He nodded at the broken case next to the shelves of wine. Carla felt herself flush when his gaze rested on her unfinished glass of tawny Port at one side.

"Another very old bottle of Port."

"You can describe it?"

Brightening, Carla said, "I took a photograph of it." She took her camera from her handbag, removed it from the case and turned it on. His eyes narrowed as he clicked through the pictures.

"You take a lot of pictures. Of this shop. Of the street. Of the bottle in the case. Of the other bottle. Why?"

"I'm an interior designer. I decorate homes," Carla explained, although her work was far more complex than that. "Photos can suggest atmosphere," she said, and then thought that sounded lame.

"Hmm. Assinado por um duque," he murmured.

"Signed by a duke? My uncle had a bottle of Port signed by a duke?" Maria peered over his arm. "Strange," she murmured. She knit her brows, turning a pensive gaze on Carla.

"Carla?" Carla was relieved to see Owen's tall, lanky frame looming in the doorway. "What's going on?" he asked.

"Espera!" Agent Cunha said, appearing at his shoulder. "You must wait outside."

But Owen strode into the shop and put his arm around Carla.

"He's my husband," she said, wishing she could lean against Owen forever and not let go.

Esteves nodded. "Okay. So. Senhora, you will come with me to the station. Your husband can come with you."

"What's going on?" Owen repeated. He peered over the counter. "Oh." In his take-charge hotel coordinator voice, he asked, "Why does my wife have to go to the station? This is a traumatic experience for her. I'd like to take her home."

"She found the body. We must take a statement."

"You can't take a statement here?"

"We must also download her pictures," Esteves said, still waggling the camera in his hand, so that Carla felt like snatching it back.

Reluctantly she gave him the camera bag as well. "Here, please put it in this. You'll be careful, won't you?"

"We know how to download pictures," Esteves said. "You will ride with me." He turned to Maria and said something in Portuguese.

Maria took a notepad from her shoulder bag and began writing furiously. To Carla, she said, "They want that I go to the station to tell them more about my uncle. Please call me. I will give you language lessons." She said the last sentence loudly, with emphasis on "language."

"That's so kind of you," Carla said, "but you mustn't trouble yourself at a time like this. I'm so sorry about your . . ." she began, then stopped as she read the note.

Below the phone number, Maria had scribbled, "Please call me, I must talk with you about my uncle."

"I do need lessons," Carla said, looking up, seeing the intensity in Maria's eyes. She put the paper in her pocket. "I was thinking of going to a language institute, but one-on-one would be so much better," She was aware she was babbling. Not that it mattered. Chief Esteves was at the door, speaking to Cunha and into his cell phone by turns. Finished, he took Maria gently by the elbow and nodded to Owen to accompany Carla.

"Do not worry, senhora," Esteves said, when she hesitated. "Only a statement. Nothing more."

In the police car, Carla and Maria sat in the back seat. Owen rode shotgun next to the police chief. Agent Cunha had remained at the shop door—closed now—waiting for the ambulance and more police to arrive. Chief Esteves was silent. But then, Carla had hardly expected him to be chatty.

Owen craned his neck around, his gray eyes clouded with concern. "I moved my meeting up to four," he told her. "I can cancel it if you want. We can talk at lunch."

31

"I could use a glass of wine," Carla said. The pleasant buzz from the Port Senhor Costa gave her had long since vanished, along with any desire for food.

She glanced over at Maria who stared stonily ahead.

"About your uncle," Carla began. But Maria gave a quick shake of the head. Despite the shock of finding Costa's corpse, Carla's interest was piqued.

A yellow ambulance with a shrieking horn zigzagged around cars and whizzed past. The huge blue letters—INEM (for Institute de Emergência Médica, according to *Living in Portugal)*—took up nearly half a panel. *Not that it matters.* Carla massaged the space between her eyebrows tiredly.

A second police car followed, its two-note siren blaring high and low, as if from an old, World War II movie. No doubt both vehicles were on their way to the shop. Carla felt her eyes get teary. She was being taken to a police station to give a statement because a nice old man who had toasted her health less than two hours ago now lay dead behind his counter.

She glanced again at her seat mate. Why did Maria want to talk about her uncle to Carla of all people? And why didn't she want the police to know?

Chapter Three - Only a Statement, Nothing More

C hief Esteves drove them down a sloping street to the station's parking area below, a plaza bordered by small buildings. An officer inside a kiosk in the center waved at him. They walked past parked police cars, slender orange trees in planters, and a row of weeping willows, which struck Carla as fitting for a police station. *Probably a number of people cry their eyes out here.*

The police chief led them inside a small building jutting out at the far left, and introduced Carla and Owen to Detetive Veríssimo Fernandes, a slim, dapper man with thinning hair and a pencil mustache that looked like it had been sketched on his long, melancholy face. After giving him Carla's camera, Esteves motioned Maria to follow him down a hall to another office.

"Please sit," Fernandes told Carla. "I think you will be more comfortable calling me 'Detective' than 'Detetive.' I am comfortable either way. They are so close, no?" He pulled out one of the chairs against the wall for her, then sat in another. Owen remained standing, arms folded against the top button of his suit jacket. After a moment, he moved behind her and gave her shoulders a comforting squeeze.

At a desk in the corner, a pretty brunette crooked a phone between her ear and shoulder, jotting notes on a sheet of paper and occasionally commenting. The soft *sh-sh* Portuguese consonants splashed into the silence, a

33

hypnotizing accompaniment to Fernandes's grave stare. Behind wire-rimmed glasses, his eyes were a startling pale blue.

"Chefe Esteves tells me you found Senhor Costa's body," he finally said. He spoke excellent English, Carla noticed, with only a faint lilt to his r's.

"Yes."

He remained silent, as if waiting for more.

"He was on the floor. Behind the counter," Carla added. She closed her eyes to shut out the memory of Costa's stare and the lump on his forehead, then opened them again when the scene only became more vivid.

"I'm sure it was disturbing," the detective said softly. "When Estela gets off the phone, you can fill out your statement at her desk while she downloads your pictures in my office. We have a coffee machine, if you would like a cup."

"Thank you, no," Carla said. The acrid flavor she normally enjoyed would probably only make her want to throw up. She felt another comforting squeeze from Owen.

Detective Fernandes rose and said, as if it were an afterthought, "And if I may see your passport . . . Do you have it with you?"

Jarred, Carla said, "Well, yes, but . . .."

Owen's hands tightened on her shoulders. "Why do you need that?" he demanded.

"I will just write down the number. A mere formality."

Wordlessly Carla took her passport out of the inner zipper-pocket in her purse and gave it to Fernandes. Her anxiety must have shown on her face.

"There is nothing to worry about," he said, but Carla noticed that he seemed to be jotting down more than the number on a notepad he took from his pocket.

"This isn't your office?" she thought to ask, as Estela hung up and disappeared into a doorway with the camera.

"A reception area," he explained. Somehow, that made Carla feel better. Just a form to fill out. No interrogation in some dark, remote room.

She sat at the desk and Detective Fernandes returned her passport and handed her the form. "Please try to remember everything," he said. "Perhaps there is some little detail you forgot to tell Chefe Esteves that will help us understand what happened." Owen sent her a supportive blink. The detective folded his hands behind his back while Carla wrote.

After filling out her and Owen's contact information, Carla scribbled down everything she could think of: The wine tasting. The phone call. The bottle in the glass case. The way Senhor Costa kept looking under the counter. The peculiar way Carla caught him watching her after bagging the bottle. Remembering it now, it seemed he said, "I will see you again" only because he knew she'd find a surprise in that bag.

Then the return. The broken case. The office door ajar to the basement. The other door onto the outside corridor. "Someone could have come in that way," she wrote, and for a moment she was sorry she hadn't tried the handle to see what was out there.

Seeing Detective Fernandes's quizzical lift of brows, Carla realized she had paused.

"I found the body," she wrote. "The welt on his forehead shocked me. It looked deliberate." She shuddered. "Like someone wanted to be sure he was dead," she wrote.

She skipped over Costa's false teeth and went to the theft of the duke's bottle when she was calling for help. "The man had been watching me. Mr. Costa's niece said he was in the shop earlier." She gave a quick description, including the scars on the thief's lip and eyebrow.

Detective Fernandes read her signed statement and gave her a curious glance. "Do you read mysteries, Senhora Bass?"

Before she could answer, he asked, "You saw no one else enter or come out of the shop?"

"Yes. I saw two men." She said slowly, remembering. "Before I went into the shop the first time."

"Would you please describe them? It would be helpful." He gave her back the form.

On the back, since she'd run out of space, Carla wrote, "A tall gray-haired man in an old-fashioned dark suit came out. Then another man, old but fashionable, went in." She described the second man's goatee and smart haircut, adding, "Both looked upset, but neither looked dangerous."

After a quick scan of her words, the detective turned his watery blue gaze on her and said, "Whether they are dangerous or not is for us to decide."

Carla felt her cheeks grow warm. "Yes, of course."

Estela returned with the camera. After a brief exchange with Fernandes in Portuguese, she gave it to Carla.

"You have been very helpful," Fernandes said. "If we have further questions, we will contact you." He gave her and Owen each a card. "This is my number if you think of anything else."

At the door, he said to Carla, "I must ask you not to leave the country until the case is closed."

"Wait just a minute," Owen said. "I have to fly to California next month to take care of some business matters."

"You may leave the country. She should not."

"But I have clients to visit," she protested.

The detective frowned at her. "I would hope there is no need to get a court order . . .."

"Am I a suspect?" Carla's voice wobbled.

"Anyone near or in the shop in connection with this unfortunate happening has our interest. Senhor Costa's niece, the man who stole the bottle, the two men you saw . . .."

"Me," Carla whispered.

"It is only routine, until this case is solved. Nothing more."

But some cases take years to solve! Carla bit her lower lip.

"I hope you solve it quickly," Owen said, a grim look on his face. He folded his arms. "My wife has no reason to kill a wine-seller. She has no reason to kill anyone." His voice rose. "She's not a killer!"

"I'm sure this is true," Detective Fernandes said, "but there are procedures."

Chapter Four – Something Weird Was Going On

Sitting at one of the tables in Centésima Página's back garden, Carla sipped the house white wine and picked at her quiche. The umbrella above cast a golden sheen on their white tablecloth.

"Not hungry?" Owen asked. "Me neither." He'd loosened his tie and draped his jacket over the chair back. His blue shirt gave his gray eyes a bluish cast. He reached over and stroked her hair back from her temple. "Babe, it's going to be all right. There must be someone we can talk to. Someone higher up."

Carla stared morosely at her plate, drawing a circle on the white tablecloth with her index finger. "It might just make things worse."

Owen lapsed into silence. After a moment, he said, "You're probably right. I suppose Fernandes knows his job, even if he's a jerk."

For a moment Carla toyed with the idea of flying out to the San Francisco office anyway. But Fernandes had mentioned a court order. There was Owen's assignment to consider. If she did something stupid, something rash, she could put him and his whole project in a bad light.

"You should eat something even if I don't." She indicated the salmon sandwich and fries on his plate.

A party of six under a blue umbrella at the next table spoke rapidly in what Carla guessed was Spanish. Their voices rose and fell in laughter—people enjoying *their* lunches, oblivious of a dead body a few streets away. She glanced at the leafy hydrangea bushes not yet in bloom on either side of the bookstore's back doorway. The caption she'd intended for the café post came to mind: "Capture the eye-catching charm of Portugal . . .."

Nothing says 'eye-catching' like a corpse. I should have stuck with the café.

Mentally she went over the scene in the wine shop again. Costa on the floor behind the counter. The lump on his forehead. The shattered case. It was the kind of thing that happened to Aimée Leduc, her favorite Parisian insurance investigator, not to Carla Bass, interior designer from the Bay Area.

"Babe, I can cancel the meeting," Owen said.

"Hmm?"

"You look exhausted. Do you want me to cook dinner?"

"I'm fine," Carla lied. Actually, she felt simultaneously drained and hyper. She forced a smile. "Well, we said we were looking forward to new venues and new adventures, right?"

He squeezed her hand. "I think we had different adventures in mind."

"True," she said ruefully. Up to now, around their work hours, Braga had been a magical place, full of romantic dinners, ardent nights, scenic tours on Sundays, when work stopped and they were free to sightsee.

Now, despite how tired she was, questions whirled in her mind. Why had Costa wanted her to look at more wine samples on the shelves while he bagged the bottle she chose?

Why had he suggested she take pictures of the Port in the glass case?

To keep me from seeing him put the duke's bottle in the bag instead of my own.

"Something weird was going on," she told Owen. "Senhor Costa switched those bottles on purpose."

Owen released her hand. "Why would he do that?"

"To get the duke's bottle out of his shop. But what made him think I'd bring it back?" she wondered aloud. "I could have just kept it."

The corner of Owen's mouth drew to one side wryly. "You have an honest face, babe. Of course you'd bring it back if it was the wrong bottle." He picked up his sandwich.

"Costa deliberately swapped them."

Owen shook his head. "Your Senhor Costa just made a mistake, babe. From what you've said, he had things on his mind, probably the bottle in the display case. That picture you showed me? Three thousand euros? Someone wanted *that* bottle, and Costa surprised him." Owen bit into his salmon.

Carla pushed her quiche to one side. "I can't finish this. I'll have a couple of your potatoes, though." She snagged a fry, following a couple of bites with another sip of wine, her thoughts returning to the wine shop.

"I'll bet anything that a bottle signed by a duke would be worth more than three thousand euros. After Senhor Costa got that phone call . . . .."

Owen's forehead crinkled in worry. "Babe, let the police handle it."

"They think *I'm* a suspect! A minute ago, you were complaining about that."

"I know. I know. Look, I don't particularly like Fernandes, but he *is* a detective. A thief already banged Costa over the head with a wine bottle. I don't want you to be next."

"How do you know the thief who took that bottle wasn't the man who stole my bottle? Well… the bottle I was returning?"

"All the more reason to let the police handle it." Owen pressed a palm against her cheek. "Go home and rest. Read one of your mysteries. No, I take that back,' he amended. "Watch a Portuguese movie on TV. You know we keep saying we'll do that. It had to be horrible to find the . . . uh, Senhor Costa. You need to get it out of your mind."

"Portuguese. I'm glad you reminded me." In a casual tone, Carla said, "I may call Maria Santos to set up language lessons." For a moment, she thought of telling him about Maria's strange message. *Later.*

"Good idea. Tell her we both want lessons, and find out what she charges," Owen said. "Seriously, though, let me cook tonight. Second offer. You gotta admit I make great fish and chips."

Carla slanted her eyes at him. "You're already having chips. Go back to work. I'm planning a surprise for you."

"Oh? Give me a hint?"

She eyed his plate. "Something better than a sandwich."

Chapter Five – What Harm Can a Little Investigating Do?

In the apartment, Carla shredded a head of kale, minced a yellow onion and a clove of garlic, sliced six potatoes, added bouillon, and brought the whole thing to boil, then turned down the flame to let it simmer. It was the first time she was trying caldo verde. Normally she thought of hot soup as being a winter dish, but the kale-and-potato soup, poured over rounds of pork sausage, was popular here in cafés all year round. She was also planning rojões cominho—braised pork cubes with cumin, coriander, lemon and wine—but she'd start that after her conference with Bethany.

Making soup always put her in a good mood. The caldo verde gave off an inviting aroma that made her stomach growl. She sliced off a heel of the bread she'd bought at the market on the way home. Nibbling it, she turned off the flame and went up the hallway to her office.

As she downloaded her pictures into the Portugal album on her computer, Costa's doorway with its beautiful blue and white azulejos conjured up the cozy alcove where he had offered her wine and crackers, both of them unaware he'd be dead before lunch. The name of the shop was tiled above the harvest scene: Adega do Costa—Costa's wine cellar. Why hadn't she checked that earlier? There was probably a website with a phone number. She might have intervened at a crucial time and stalled whatever was about to happen.

The phone call Costa had received while she was in the shop still nagged at her. On a hunch, she thumbed through *621 Portuguese Verbs*. She was sure Senhor Costa had said, "não o tenho—I don't have it." Not "não o quero—I don't want it."

She was right. And "it" had to have been the bottle that the duke signed.

So, who was Senhor Costa talking to? The creepy man who stole it from her when she was looking for help? After killing Costa, had he hung around to see what would happen next? Carla had read about killers watching the action afterwards, even helping the police search for suspects. It could explain why the thief was waiting across the street when she rushed out of the shop.

She turned on her laptop and entered "antique Port wines" into Google. Maybe some background on the duke's bottle would explain why Senhor Costa had it in the first place. A lot of sites came up, many about wine auctions. She clicked through them, but none of the Ports were what she was looking for. She rested her elbows on her desk and her chin on her hands, thinking.

Senhor Costa would have switched bottles when she was photographing the one in the case. Whoever called him must have said he was coming right over. But he didn't find the bottle because she had it. Costa probably thought the caller would be convinced and go away. *But what did Costa plan to do with the Port when I returned it?*

What would someone do with a bottle that had a label signed by a duke? It hadn't been in the glass case with the other bottle. He must have had special plans for it. Carla pulled up her album pictures of the bottle again. Duque C. J. – maybe Carlos José or Carlos Juan – of Acaer. 1863.

"Obrigado." That meant "Thank you." Actually, it meant "Obligated." Duque C. J. felt obligated to someone for something. Who was Duque C. J.?

She fed "Duque Carlos José" into Google, and dozens of partial names came up: Duque José, Duque Carlos, José Duque, Carlos Duque; some in Spain; some in France. A lot of them were on Facebook, which made her smile. She tried combinations with Juan. After a few minutes, she gave it up and wondered if she could look up Senhor Costa instead. She didn't know his first name. But she had the name of the shop. She typed in Adega do Costa and clicked her mouse. A list of restaurants and bars came up, but no website for a wine shop.

The warbling tone of Skype interrupted her thoughts.

"Hey, what's up?" Bethany wanted to know. "You're usually right on the dot. I have some interesting news."

Carla looked at her menu bar. Ten after six. "I was . . . doing some research."

Bethany's forehead puckered with concern. "Everything okay?"

"Sure. Why?"

"I don't know. You look kinda frazzled."

Carla glanced at the small video of herself in the lower corner. Her long, blonde hair was tangled. She hadn't thought to comb it. Her face seemed washed out and tense. Her lipstick was eaten off. "It's been an unusual day."

"Unusual how?"

Carla hesitated.

"You and Owen aren't having problems, are you?" Bethany's large brown eyes widened in worried sympathy.

"No, we're good."

"You'd tell me if something was the matter, right, honey?" Bethany had grown up in Beverly Hills, influenced by Hollywood, and "honey" still wove through her conversations, even though she'd been in the Bay Area for twenty years.

"You know I would," Carla assured her. They told each other everything. They'd met at California College of the Arts in the nineties—California College of Arts and Crafts at the time—and they'd clicked right away. They double dated with boyfriends, consoled each other over break-ups, compared courses at the college, and later compared the different businesses where they interned. It was during their internships they discovered they had a similar vision for what an interior design business should be like. Their look would be classical elegance. Traditional. Nothing modern. Ten years ago, their combined savings and a bank loan had enabled them to open Traditional Home Atmospheres in SoMa—the South of Market Area of San Francisco. The loan had long since been paid off, and the business was doing well.

"So, if it's not Owen..." Bethany said.

"I'll tell you after biz talk, okay? Let's get the week lined up. You said you have some interesting news?"

Bethany hooked a lock of her short, auburn hair behind her ear. "New client," she said. "Guess where? Carmel."

"Nice!" Carla loved that whole area. She and Owen had honeymooned in Carmel. Her birthday present for him last year had been a gift card to play at Pebble Beach Golf Links.

"Name's Jeffery B. Gage," Bethany said. *Is that a sparkle in her eye?* "I'll be driving down to meet with him at the house Wednesday and do a walk through while we go over plans. He's sent pictures of it. French Provincial now, but he's thinking Victorian. I already have some ideas."

Meet with him. Not with them. "Sounds like our new client's single. A widower?"

"Recently divorced." Bethany gave a brittle laugh. "I remember what that's like." Her own brief marriage had broken up two years ago, and for a while Carla had worried about the hard shell of cynicism Bethany was developing. But lately she had seemed to be coming out of her doldrums, even to the point of exploring online dating.

"Does he have English ancestors or something?" Carla asked. "Why Victorian?"

Bethany shrugged. "Clean sweep thing? Wife liked one look, he's going for another? You know, either get rid of the memories or move." Bethany had sold the house and moved into an apartment.

"Do you have a color scheme in mind?"

"I'm thinking wine and ivory, some forest green, some gold touches. Maybe wine velvet for the sofa and wing chairs. Fabric wallpaper in some rooms. Patterned carpets. Lots of moldings. That sort of thing."

Carla nodded. "Holly can check out fabrics and wallpapers." Holly was one of their junior designers. "How authentic does he want the furniture? Is he into antiques?"

"I think he's fine with some reproductions and a few real pieces. What he wants is 'the look.' Dark wood in the library, glassed-in shelves for special books. Atrium with a potted fern."

Carla was curious. "How did he hear of us?"

"He saw the spread last month in *Traditional Home.* The one on the remodel we did in San Mateo? His receptionist saw it, anyway."

46

"So, what does our new and wealthy client do?" He had to be wealthy, remodeling a home in Carmel.

"He's an oral surgeon."

"Better keep your smile bright."

Bethany laughed. "Any big discoveries at your end?"

Big discoveries. Carla tried not to think of Senhor Costa. "I talked to Filomena at the auction house in Porto. Given the budget Mrs. Demming gave us, I'm pretty sure my bid will get the Da Silva Porto paintings Thursday," she said. "I already made prearrangements to have them picked up Saturday and delivered to Porto Monday. And I've made arrangements for the stone cherub to go sea freight. It should be shipped sometime next week. Oh, and I saw a nice gilt-framed mirror today that would look great in Mrs. Demming's hallway. I'm emailing a picture of it to her. If she likes it, I'll include it with her paintings and arrange to send them and the statue to Belvedere."

"Sounds good." Bethany was jotting things on her notepad. "By the way," she said, "your blog was a good idea. A Mr. and Mrs. Duarte came across your post about tiles while browsing our website. They own a restaurant in Oakland, but want to revamp their home in the Oakland hills. They're wondering if we could do their entrance in azulejos. It's a heritage thing. His grandfather came over from the Azores, I think, and had a creamery in San Leandro."

"That's it? Just the entrance?"

"So far."

"Hmm. See if you can talk them into doing the bathrooms in azulejos, too. That could be stunning. I can check with a few places in Porto that make them."

Bethany nodded. "I'll make an appointment to meet with them and arrange for someone to be at Mrs. Demming's home when things get delivered. Let me know dates." She looked up from her scribbling. "That it?"

"More or less. I'll have all the bills sent later this week."

"So . . ." Bethany leaned in closer to the computer as if they were across a table from each other in the same room. "What's this research you're doing?"

"I found a dead man today."

"Excuse me?" The pen Bethany had been tapping came to a halt. "You found . . . did you say a *dead man?*"

"In a shop where I was buying a bottle of Port."

"Oh, my God!"

While Carla recounted what happened. Bethany listened as if riveted to the spot. No one could listen the way Bethany could, which made her Carla's "go-to" friend after Owen for hashing out concerns. She wished Bethany were closer. Skyping wasn't the same as talking in person.

"I'd still like to know who was after him," Carla said. "He switched bottles, right? He knew someone was coming. Probably the guy that stole it from me after disposing of the other bottle."

"Let the police handle it, honey," Bethany said.

"Who says I'm not?" Carla said.

"You have a gleam in your eye. And you said you were doing research."

"What harm can a little investigating do?"

"On a man who's just been killed? And his niece wants to talk to you without the police knowing? Not good, Carla."

"Wouldn't *you* want to know why?"

"No. I wouldn't. Not with a killer on the loose. Keep out of it, honey. You're in a strange land. You don't even know the language."

"All the more reason to let Maria give me language lessons. Besides," Carla added, "it seems I'm a person of interest."

"A person of interest!"

"Yeah. A suspect."

"That's ridiculous!"

"Hey, they asked me not to leave the country until the case is solved."

"You've gotta be kidding!"

"'Fraid not." Carla waved a hand dismissively. "It's just procedure," she said, hoping Fernandes meant what he said. "Our dauntless detective *must* follow procedures."

Bethany's own curiosity seemed to get the best of her. "You say one bottle was taken that was worth three thousand euros?" Carla nodded. "And the other, the one taken from you, was signed by a duke?" Carla nodded again. "That's probably worth thirty thousand at least, don't you think?"

"A lot, anyway," Carla pressed her lips together. *Enough to kill for?* "I have pictures of both bottles," she said. "And the shop. Oh. And the mirror I told you about? Hang on, I'll show them to you." She opened her photo album again, clicked "share," then showed Bethany the photos, one by one.

Bethany whistled. "They don't even look like normal bottles, do they! Exquisite labels, I have to say. And the tile over the doorway is gorgeous."

"I was thinking of posting it on our website," Carla said. "But now I don't think so. It doesn't feel right, after what's happened."

49

"Yeah. You're right. Mrs. Demming will love the mirror, though."

"I think so." Carla looked at the menu bar again and saw the time. "Oops, I'd better go. Gotta finish cooking dinner. This dish is a little complicated."

"I hope when you guys come back you remember normal eating hours. I don't see how you can eat so late."

"If you took a long weekend and visited us, you'd understand."

"Ha-ha. You know me and flying. New York, I can do. Anything over the big ocean? No way. That's why you get Europe, right?"

"I thought it was because Owen had a hotel assignment," Carla teased. She had actually made several trips in the past to Paris for French antiques. "Okay, talk again, Friday?"

A furrow appeared between Bethany's eyebrows. "Be careful, honey."

"Of course, I'll be careful. There's nothing to worry about." Later Carla was to remember how easily she said that.

After they hung up, she e-mailed Mrs. Demming the mirror picture, then tried Maria's phone.

"Olá," Carla said in Portuguese when Maria answered, pretending to herself this was about language lessons and not about Maria's cloak-and-dagger behavior.

"Oh, it is you, senhora." Maria's voice was low, confidential, as if she didn't want someone to hear. "I will meet you tomorrow morning at the Jardim de Santa Bárbara, yes? Ten o'clock, before I go to class. You can come, yes?"

"Well, I . . . I," Carla stammered, taken aback by how take-charge Maria seemed. "I suppose so."

"Very good. You know where it is?"

50

"It's not far from where I live," Carla said. Five streets away, the 17th-century gardens tucked behind the former Archbishop's Court were a major tourist attraction, with various blooms in season planted among roses and sculpted boxwoods.

"Good. Thank you, senhora. Obrigada." Maria's voice turned surprisingly cheery. "I see you at ten." She hung up.

"Well," Carla murmured in the empty apartment. "What was that all about?" Feeling a little shiver of adventure, she went into the tiled kitchen and began cubing the pork.

Chapter Six – In the Jardim de Santa Bárbara

The next morning, Carla stared out the French doors that led to the balcony from the sala de estar—literally, the "being room" in Portuguese. She sipped her second cup of coffee, mulling over the coming meeting. It irked her that Maria Santos had so easily manipulated the time and place. Normally she was the one who took charge with clients. *Okay, so I called her, not vice versa.* She guessed that put her in client mode. *And it wasn't really about language lessons.* Snoop that she was, Carla couldn't resist finding out what Maria had to say about Costa.

She took a new sip of her cafezinho, a dark, rich coffee fixed the Brazilian way. Owen had left for work an hour ago. She'd already received Mrs. Demming's e-mail saying she wanted the mirror. So that was one matter taken care of.

Across the street, a woman at the balcony above the barber shop was watering her pink geraniums again. She wore a bright yellow, bibbed apron embroidered with red flowers, the kind of apron Nana would have loved, if she were still alive. Carla's grandmother had raised her after her parents died in a car crash when she was fourteen. Even now, Carla felt herself easing carefully around a pain that throbbed when she remembered the moment she'd been called to the principal's office, wondering if she were in trouble. Instead, Nana had been waiting, her eyes red from crying. She put her arms around Carla as she broke the news that Mom and Dad were gone. The small Victorian house Carla had grown up in on Potrero Hill in San Francisco was sold soon after, and she went to live in her grandmother's antique-filled brown-shingled home in Berkeley. Nana had always been a doting grandmother, but after the accident she became a friend as well, helping Carla navigate her grief and adjust to a new future.

How Nana would have loved Braga!

She blinked regret away and waved at her neighbor across the way. The woman waved back before going inside, and Carla made a mental note to go over one day and get acquainted. Better yet, invite her over for coffee.

If she speaks English. "Bom dia" only went so far.

A young man sauntered from the direction of Igreja de São Victor a street away. There were so many churches in the historic section, Carla had started using them as location markers. She studied his slight frame. *A teenager on his way to school.* His lightweight, beige hoodie hid his face. She watched him continue past the barber shop and cross the next street, head bobbing up and down as if in time to music—no doubt from ear buds under his hood. From time to time, he peered at buildings, as if looking for an address. House numbers were visible enough on doorways, but street names were on metal plaques or carved in stone plaques, and not always at street corners. Maybe he was looking for a new girlfriend's address. Maybe he wasn't on his way to school but skipping class.

She shrugged, took her cup into the kitchen and rinsed it out, then set it in the wire rack on the granite counter. Through the window, she could hear church bells echoing each other, reminding her to leave soon if she didn't want to be late.

On her way to the door, the cell phone on the hall table warbled. Probably Owen wanting her to bring by something he forgot. Instead it was Detective Fernandes.

"Senhora Bass?" he asked, his voice quiet and polite.

Carla put a fist on her hip. *Sound as courteous as you want, buddy.* After his don't-leave-the-country gambit yesterday, she didn't trust him.

"Yes?" she said, matching his polite tone.

"Senhora, I am Detetive Fernandes."

"I recognized your voice."

"*Detec*tive Fernandes, if that is easier for you," he continued smoothly.

Maybe she was being too harsh. Besides, he might have good news. "Have you found out who killed Senhor Costa?"

"I would like to speak with you." *So, probably not.* "It may take some time. Do you wish to come to the station, or shall I come to your home?"

Carla hesitated. She could probably call Maria and change their meeting time. But since she didn't know what this was about, she'd prefer Owen to be present. "I'm late for an appointment," she said. "Can you come to our apartment this evening?"

Detective Fernandes was silent a moment before asking, "What is a good time for you?"

Owen would be home around six-forty-five. They could have leftovers after Fernandes left. "How about seven this evening?"

"Very good. Seven." The detective hung up. A focused man, obviously, who didn't waste time on niceties.

Carla slipped on her blazer, put her phone in her handbag and left. As she turned from locking the street door, she saw the woman across was on her balcony again, enjoying a smoke. Sunlight glinted on her shoulder-length, wavy hair, bringing out its auburn tones. Smiling, she called to Carla in a thick accent, "Good morning. You are English, yes?"

"American," Carla called.

"How you like our city?"

"I love it."

"It is beautiful place, yes?"

Carla nodded. *When bodies aren't lying around in wine shops.*

"What is your name? We must get to know each other. I am Natália. Natália Freitas."

"Carla Bass. I'd love that. But right now," Carla tapped her watch, "I have an appointment. Later this week, maybe?"

"Very good."

Walking briskly to the bank next to Owen's hotel, Carla was pleased. In her and Owen's Piedmont home, she knew all her neighbors. It was one aspect of being away from home that she missed. It would be nice to have a local friend in Braga. Someone to have coffee with, gossip with.

She crossed Rua da Chãos, which teemed with buses and delivery vans. From there it was a short zigzag to the Santa Bárbara gardens, which were actually a group of four manicured squares defined by boxwood hedges and topiaries and filled with rose bushes. Beds of purple and yellow pansies edged each section. Wide paths led to a central fountain topped by the gray stone statue of Santa Bárbara whose face tilted slightly up, as if in supplication.

At the end of one path, on a stone bench near the fountain, Maria Santos sat slump-shouldered, staring into space, a newspaper spread on her lap, her book bag at her side. Carla made her way down the path and sat beside her.

"Sorry I'm late. Have you been here long?"

Maria smiled wanly. Her wavy dark hair fell around her face. She wore a long-sleeved tee and blue jeans. A scarf was knotted at her throat, making her look casually fashionable. She indicated the newspaper. "I was reading . . ." Her voice trailed off.

"Is that today's paper?" At Maria's nod, Carla asked, "What does it say?"

"Only a little." Maria showed her the page with its photo of a younger Senhor Costa, looking devilishly handsome. There was also a picture of the 1812, three-thousand-euro Port in the case—*my photo*, Carla noted—and another photo of the empty smashed case.

"Uh, since I don't read Portuguese . . .."

"Oh. I am sorry. It says a customer comes into the shop and found my uncle dead, and this rare bottle of Port is stolen. They investigate. He is well-liked by other business owners in the neighborhood. The police contact . . . are contacting his family."

"They didn't mention who the customer was who discovered him?"

"No."

And why would they? "They didn't mention a second bottle was stolen?"

"No."

Carla thought of the men she'd seen going in and out of the shop yesterday. "Nothing about two other men who went into the shop?"

Maria shook her head.

Maybe the police don't want suspects to realize they're suspects.

Curious, she asked, "Did you see those men?"

"Customers always go into the shop," Maria said. "I didn't notice anyone except . . .." She fell silent.

Except who? Carla's curiosity tingled. "You must be so upset about your uncle," she prompted.

"Yes. I have phoned my mother last night. He was her brother. I have also called his wife, because she will arrange the funeral. It will be here in Braga." Maria folded the newspaper and tucked it into her book bag.

"She must be terribly upset, too."

"Not really." Maria made a little moue. "They did not live together for many years. They did not get along. She will only be interested how much money he leaves."

"I see," Carla murmured, thinking she probably didn't. Portugal was a very Catholic country and Braga one of its most conservative cities. "I suppose divorce was out of the question."

"She did not want to be divorced, even though they make . . . made each other unhappy."

With a surge of sympathy for Senhor Costa, Carla said, "He must have had a lonely life."

Maria said in a tight voice. "He had another woman."

"Oh." In Portuguese, the word for "woman" was also a word for "wife." Was Senhor Costa a bigamist? Carla decided not. Another wife would probably have to live in another town. His other woman must be his mistress.

"Senhora Bass . . .."

"Call me Carla."

"I cannot. It is not polite. You are older."

"Not that much older," Carla protested. "I'm only thirty-six." When Maria still looked hesitant, she said, "I insist."

"Very well." Maria folded her hands. "Carla." She sent Carla a shy glance. "Thirty-six? Do you have children?"

Carla caught her breath. "Not yet," she said after a pause. She made her voice cheerful. "There are still things we want to do. More travel. And we both like our careers."

She and Owen had decided in November they were ready to start a family. When she went off the pill, she'd expected to become pregnant right away, but that didn't happen. Tests didn't reveal a reason, but her doctor reassured her it was too early for her to think of fertility treatments. "If you haven't conceived after a year," she said, "then we can consider some options. Often the problem just corrects itself. Enjoy your life. Relax. Let nature take its course."

Coming to Portugal had seemed a lucky way to follow her advice: The atmosphere in Braga was so laid back, Carla could feel the rushed tension of Bay Area living drift out of her day by day.

Until yesterday.

Still, by the time they returned home, she hoped she'd be shopping for baby clothes.

Maria's voice broke into her thoughts. "I don't think I will have children for a long time. I am like you. I will have business and travel."

Carla pushed the issue of family to the back of her mind and considered Maria's mysterious note. *Start with the language lessons.* "I really do need someone to help me learn Portuguese," she said. "I get the grammar. But the pronunciation is killing me."

58

Maria laughed. With a touch of pride, she said, "Our language is difficult, yes? I can come to your home. And perhaps you will help me with my English."

Okay, fine. Now, let's get back to the uncle.

"In your note, you said," Carla began.

On the street, a group of young girls, their voices rising and falling in sibilant consonants and nasalized vowels, made their way toward the Pastelaria Lusitana.

"When I travel, I will go to Brazil," Maria said, "after I finish my studies in Lusofonia."

"Lusofonia?" Carla asked, aware she was losing control of the conversation again.

"The study of all Portuguese speaking countries and their cultures. Did you know that the Portuguese in Brazil is different from—"

"In your note, you said you wanted to tell me about your uncle," Carla interrupted.

"Sim. Yes." Maria's face immediately became grave. She glanced down at her hands.

"What about your uncle?" Carla asked when the silence between them lengthened.

Maria turned to her, her dark eyes sad. "I want you to find out who killed him."

Carla stared. "I'm sure the police are doing that," she said.

"My uncle was not a good man, but he was not a bad man. He did not deserve to be killed."

"The police will take care of it."

Maria didn't reply.

"Why wasn't he a good man?" Carla asked gently. *Aside from having two women?*

Maria colored with embarrassment. "He like to gamble. One time he tries . . . tried to cheat in cards. He bet a special bottle of Port, but he doesn't want to pay, so he cheated, but the person he was cheating caught him."

A bottle of Port? Carla perked up. "Was it the bottle he kept in the glass case?"

"No, some other bottle. He finally gives . . . gave it to the man. But I am ashamed he would cheat."

"How do you know all this?"

"One of my friends that I share the apartment with. Ana. She works part time as maid for the widow of this man he gave the Port to. She—the widow—is angry when Ana mentions my uncle's wine shop and says she knows me."

"That seems a little extreme."

"After my uncle gave the Port to the woman's husband, they were never friends again. I don't think my parents know this. I only find out when Ana came to room with us. I was so much disappointed."

"But that's not what you wanted to tell me about your uncle," Carla said. It was a less admirable side of Senhor Costa than she would have expected, but if he had paid up, it was hardly a reason to kill him after all this time.

"My uncle was worried about something. I am trying to think what."

"You should let the police handle it," Carla said, aware that it was what both Owen and Bethany had told her.

"But yesterday I didn't tell you all the truth."

Carla narrowed her eyes. "About what?"

"I did see someone go into the shop before you came with your bottle."

"Oh?" Carla heard her voice turn cold and distant.

"Just before you went inside the store, and before that man who stole your bottle went in and came out, Paulo also went in and came out right away, so fast he cannot have killed my uncle."

"Wait," Carla said. She put her hands to her temple. "Who is Paulo?"

"Paulo is my boyfriend."

"You've told the police about him, right?"

"No."

"Why not?"

Maria chewed at a fingernail. "They will not be fair to him."

"Why not? How can you be sure he didn't have something to do with your uncle's death?" Carla braced herself for a hot defense of the boyfriend.

Instead, Maria said mildly, "He didn't have time to kill my uncle. We were supposed to meet for lunch."

"Say that again?"

"I came early to the café and then to say hello to my uncle before to meet Paulo for lunch at Centésima Página. It is a nice bookstore with a small cafeteria."

"Yes, I know," Carla said impatiently.

"But then I looked out the window and saw Paulo goes into my uncle's shop. I wondered, 'What is he doing there? And he ran out again, in just segundos; *seconds*, I mean." Maria bit her lip. "Minutes, maybe. But only very few."

Carla stared at the stone steps leading up to the saint's statue. "So, you're saying your uncle was dead when Pablo—"

"Paulo," Maria corrected.

". . . when Paulo went inside?"

61

"Yes. And then I saw you. And then I saw the man steal the bottle from you. I even saw him go in before you came. But he came out again very fast, too."

"Why don't you tell the police all of that?"

"I told them about the thief. And about you. But Paulo cannot prove how long he was in the shop. Only I saw him, and I am his girlfriend. They will say, 'Of course you take his side.'"

While Carla mulled that over, the group of girls she had seen earlier walked back from the café, one of them laughing so hard she was gasping for breath as they went on their way.

"Why tell me all this?" Carla asked, while the practical part of her mind told her inner snoop to mind her own business.

"I have tried to call Paulo many times, but there is no answer."

Hadn't Detective Fernandes said anyone in or near the shop around the time of Senhor Costa's death was a suspect? Maybe Paulo thought he was in trouble, even if the police didn't know about him yet.

Maria added, "Paulo is a waiter at Nossa Cozinha. It is on Rua de Baixo. Can you go there tonight to see if he is working? If he is not, then something has happened to him."

"Why can't you go?" Carla asked.

"He doesn't like me to go to the restaurant. Once I had went there and he was angry with me and told me not to come again."

Carla chose her words carefully. "If Paulo is in trouble and doesn't answer his phone, he may want you to keep out of this." *And if he doesn't like you coming to his work place, kiddo, the romance is probably over.*

"So, you will not help." Maria turned her face away and flicked her long hair over her shoulder, her shoulders rigid.

"I didn't say I wouldn't help," Carla hedged. "I'm just saying you should be careful and that you should go to the police. How did you meet this Paulo, anyway?"

"He was in the wine shop one day, talking to my uncle. And later I see him in Centésima Página. He recognizes me and we start talking. As you say, small world, no?"

A suspiciously small world. "I don't know what he looks like," Carla pointed out. Not that she was going to get involved.

Maria's face lit in a smile. She took her cell phone from her pocket. "Here is his picture." The small rectangle showed a muscular young man with dark brown hair, puppy-dog eyes, sensuous lips, a faint cleft in his chin, and whorls of hair above an opened shirt button.

"Good-looking," Carla said, and refrained from adding, "in the way your mother should worry about."

Maria's eyes shone. "Pretty, yes? Handsome, I mean. You say handsome for a man, no?"

"Checking to see if he's at the restaurant won't explain who killed your uncle."

"No. This is true. But . . . .." Maria's face was awash with conflicting emotions.

Her boyfriend's alibi is as important as finding her uncle's killer?

"If you see Paulo is at work, and tell me, then I will know he is okay," Maria said.

Not gonna happen, kiddo.

"And then I will keep calling him until he answers." Maria frowned. "And ask him why he was in my uncle's shop."

"Why wouldn't he be?"

"He gets his wine from a store below his apartment. Garrafeira do Faria."

Carla knitted her brows. Something didn't add up. "Didn't you say he saw you the first time in your uncle's shop?"

"I think he only went only that once. He likes Garrafeira do Faria better."

"You probably told Paulo you often stopped by to say hello to your uncle. It seems logical he would come to your uncle's shop again, hoping to see you there."

"Paulo goes to work at eight," Maria said. "You can go in there for even a snack. They serve snacks." Church bells began tolling. She looked at her wristwatch and jumped up, gathering her book bag and handbag. "Eleven. I must go to class. The bus takes fifteen minutes and one comes soon. You will call me and tell me, yes?"

"Sit down," Carla said. "I'm not going to spy on your boyfriend for you. If you're so concerned, go to his apartment." Maria blushed, and Carla pressed her point. "If he works nights, he's bound to be home, sleeping late." Most restaurants and bars closed around one or two a.m. "What time is your class?" she asked.

"Not until three, but I will eat in the cafeteria on campus, and then I will go to one of the libraries for my research."

"I'm sure busses to the campus run pretty often. Anyway, this is something you'll have to handle on your own. There's nothing I can do." Carla rose.

"I cannot go to his apartment," Maria said, fingering the strap of her handbag.

"You were planning to keep calling him," Carla said. "Visiting is hardly worse."

"He will be angry with me that I come."

Carla folded her arms and twiddled her fingers against her elbows. *This is so not my business.* A quick glance at Maria's downcast face yanked at her. She knew what it was like to be young and in love with the wrong guy—something she had gone through in her senior year in high school, when her hunky boyfriend had gotten a cheerleader pregnant. And, except for stopping by the antique store to confirm she wanted the mirror, the day was free.

"I'll go with you," she said. "You can see for yourself if he's okay. You can ask why he was in the shop." *Something I wouldn't mind knowing myself.* Since Detective Fernandes had as much as told Carla she was a suspect until the case was closed, this might move things along.

"Maybe it is better than calling," Maria murmured.

Carla took Maria's elbow and pulled her to her feet. "Let's go."

Chapter Seven - A Visit to Paulo

Rua Jorge Araullo, four streets away from Carla's street, was in a less charming area. No tiles or bright plaster. No balconies with flowers. The paint peeling off the door of Garrafeira do Faria next to the entrance of Paulo's living quarters didn't raise any expectations for his taste in wine.

She followed Maria up two flights of narrow stairs at the back, dimly lit by low-voltage bulbs with plastic shades. On the second floor, a hall led to the front of the building. Maria knocked on a door that looked like it could use a refinishing job. After a long silence, while Maria anxiously massaged her forehead, the door opened, and a bleary-eyed Paulo peered out.

As soon as he saw Maria, he grimaced and held out a raised palm, saying something rapidly in Portuguese in a choked voice.

He started to close the door, but Carla inserted her foot, wincing, as she felt the squeeze. She pushed the door open and walked in, her stilettos clicking on the red tile floor. The apartment reeked of stale cigarettes. Other than that, it looked fairly tidy.

"Quem é ela?" Paulo asked Maria.

Carla had memorized enough of the who-what-where-why-how words to understand his question. "I'm Maria's friend," she told him, although acquaintance was probably more like it.

"You must speak English, Paulo," Maria said. "She is here to help you."

Carla lifted her brows. That was probably going too far. She eyed Paulo in his brown fleece robe. He was as handsome as the picture Maria had shown her, despite his tousled hair and his need of a morning shave. The expression that flitted across his face looked as lovelorn as Maria's.

"You must leave," he told them. "Is not safe here."

"I saw you at my uncle's shop yesterday," Maria said.

He heaved a sigh and looked at the floor.

"My uncle is dead."

He murmured something and tried to cradle her cheek in his palm, but she drew back.

"And the police questioned me."

Paulo's eyes widened. "Did you tell them you saw me?"

"No, but you must tell me why you were there."

"I was . . . looking for advice on wine."

"I don't believe you. You say you always go to Faria."

Carla walked past the green sofa to the window to give them some privacy, then realized, as Paulo lapsed back into Portuguese, he wasn't worried about her eavesdropping.

The window looked out on Rua Jorge Araullo. It occurred to Carla they were right over the drab wine shop. She turned around, impressed by the apartment's layout and decor.

Despite the building's dull exterior and the stale air inside, the place was cheery. It was all one large, airy space, wallpapered in yellow and divided by a U-shaped, yellow-tiled counter with two stools. She noticed a nearly empty bottle of wine on the counter next to an overflowing ashtray.

She went over and peered behind the counter, discovering a mini kitchenette with a two-burner range, a small refrigerator, and a tiny sink. Someone had planned it well. In the space beyond, to the right, a bed hugged the wall, its striped green spread echoing the green sofa in the lounge area. Next to the bed was an oak chest of drawers. Partly-smoked cigarettes spilled over another ashtray on the floor. A tiny hall led to what must be the bathroom. A nice finishing touch would have been some framed abstracts or travel posters, but even with bare walls and Paulo's smokes, it was an attractive little apartment.

Her glance fell on the wine bottle's label--an expensive red; Conceito Douro, 2007. Paulo had good taste in wines for someone who needed advice.

Their voices were rising. Suddenly Maria broke into English.

"Don't say that! You *are* good for me. And speak English."

She turned to Carla. "Carla, you must convince him to go to the police. He knows something he doesn't tell me. It can be dangerous for him, I think."

More than anything, Carla wanted to rewind the past half-hour. Return to that moment when she told Maria she would have to handle the problem of Paulo herself. But no, here she was in the middle of things after her smarter self told her not to get involved.

Maria and Paulo were waiting for her to speak, Maria clasping her hands, her face trustful, as if she expected Carla to magically persuade Paulo.

But what if he did it, kiddo?

Carla turned to Paulo. "Even if you were in the shop for only a few minutes," she said, "you might have noticed some little detail that could help the police." *Some little detail.* She sounded just like Detective Fernandes!

"I notice only a broken case and a dead body."

Maria beamed. "Then there is nothing to worry about."

Paulo ran his hand through his tousled hair. "I have much to worry about. I cannot speak with the police."

"If you go to the police," Carla said, curious about what he was holding back, "it will remove suspicion."

"Is not so simple. I . . . I have done something." At Maria's shocked expression, he hastened to say, "I did not kill your uncle. But I have done something, and an evil man came here this morning." Paulo massaged his bristled chin. "He will come back. I know." What he said next in Portuguese made Maria gasp and put both hands to her lips.

To Carla he said, "You both must go and not come back. Is not safe."

When neither of them budged, he flung his hands up in exasperation, turned, strode across the living space to the small hallway, and went into the bathroom. A moment later Carla heard the click of a lock and the sound of the shower.

Well. That's one way to get rid of unwanted visitors.

They continued to wait a few silent minutes, but it became clear he wasn't coming out until they were gone. For a moment, a stubborn streak in Carla made her want to open and close the apartment door loudly and then keep waiting. But what if he got physical and threw them out bodily, one by one? He looked strong enough to do that.

"We'd better go," she told Maria. On leaving, she did close the door loudly behind them so Paulo wouldn't have to keep showering for the rest of the morning. Maria pushed in front of her, holding a hand to her face. As they made their way down the hallway and stairwell, Carla could see the girl's hunched shoulders shaking while she wept.

Outside again on the pavement, Carla handed her a tissue from her handbag. "That last bit in Portuguese . . . what did he say?" she asked, as Maria dabbed at her eyes and wiped her nose.

Maria took a deep breath. "He told me I must forget I ever knew him." Another small sob came out like a hiccup. "Oh, Carla, why is life is so hard?"

First her uncle. Then her boyfriend. Carla squeezed her shoulder in sympathy. "You found out what you wanted to know," she said softly. "Paulo *is* in trouble. Serious trouble, it sounds like. No matter how difficult, you should take his advice."

The scene upstairs had brought back Carla's common sense. Owen and Bethany were right. This was a police matter. "If he won't go to the police, you need to," she told Maria. "Otherwise they'll think you're a part of whatever he's involved in."

Maria only shook her head and wiped her eyes again.

"Let me get you lunch before you catch the bus," Carla said. They were walking toward Rua de São Victor.

"I am not hungry."

"You'll feel better if you eat something."

Maria shook her head again, and Carla remembered her own lack of appetite after the shock of finding Costa. When they reached the corner, she offered, "Can I drive you to campus? We can walk back to my apartment and get the car."

"Thank you, but I must do some thinking to myself, alone. The bus is good for that." Maria indicated with her chin the bus stop to the left, halfway down the street.

"I suppose so," Carla said. "You'll be okay, then?"

"You are very kind, Carla. I have much appreciation. I will talk to you soon."

Very kind, my foot, Carla thought, watching Maria's forlorn figure walk to the stop. Guilt wrapped around her shoulders like a soggy blanket. After all, it had been her idea to go to Paulo's apartment.

Chapter Eight - Detective Fernandes Comes Calling

Detective Veríssimo Fernandes arrived three minutes after Owen finished his cigarette on the balcony, precisely at seven, accompanied by the peal of the bells from Igreja dos Congregados and Sé Catedral. He carried a black leather briefcase. After shaking hands with Owen, then Carla, he followed them into the living area. Carla led him to the overstuffed easy chair at the end of the coffee table, then sat nervously beside Owen on the nubby white sofa. He took her hand in his as the detective cleared his throat.

"Senhora Bass, I have a few questions," Fernandes leaned forward and gave her the ghost of a polite smile. Behind the wire rims, his pale blue eyes seemed fathomless.

"She wrote out a statement," Owen reminded him. "Isn't that enough?"

"Facts raise more questions, Senhor Bass. When I saw the label with the duke's signature, it triggered my memory. I remembered an article in *O Examinador* a few years ago. Three years, to be exact. I went to the newspaper office yesterday, and I looked through their archives. Your pictures were a great help, senhora."

Gratified, Carla moved Detective Fernandes a few pegs up on her approval scale. "Thank you," she said, and smiled at Owen.

"I found the article I remembered," Fernandes continued. He opened his briefcase and took out two photocopied pages, laying them on the coffee table so that they faced Carla and Owen. "Do you recognize anyone in these pictures?"

Carla picked up the first page, a reportage in Portuguese of some special event. The camera showed a clean-shaven older man with white-streaked hair and sideburns sitting below a huge painting. His cheeks had a sculpted look, almost chiseled. With apparent pride, he held a bottle, his forefinger resting just below Duke C. J. de Acaer's thank you and flourished signature. Despite the gray tonality of the news photo, Carla recognized the bottle she'd tried to return to Costa. In the painting above, an even older-looking man with a tufty mustache sat in a similar posture holding the same bottle. Above the small bow tie and white stand-up collar, his face wore a look of haughty dignity. The bottle must be some family legacy.

"The original photos and painting were in color, of course," Fernandes said.

Carla set the page down and picked up the second one. A new photo showed the bottle's owner proudly holding it in one hand toward the photographer so that the label was clear. His other arm was around the shoulder of the goateed man Carla had seen entering Costa's shop yesterday. *Leaving in a huff,* she remembered. Both smiled into the camera.

"That's one of the men I told you about," Carla told Fernandes. "He was at the auction preview last week, too."

Owen peered over her shoulder and started reading the caption aloud, "Inácio Herberto Luis Vitore, viticultor e amigo." At Fernandes's pained expression, Carla could tell Owen was murdering every word.

73

"Who is he?" she asked. "And who's the other man?"

"I am here to ask questions, senhora, not answer them."

Carla pressed her lips together. *Your approval rating just took a serious dip, buddy.*

"With all due respect," Owen said in the tone she'd heard him use on the phone when he smoothed over difficulties, "We're helping you every way we can. Don't we deserve a few answers?"

Fernandes hesitated. With a reluctance that suggested he was breaking protocol, he said, "Senhor Vitore is a vintner in the Douro valley. He lives in Porto, but he is from Braga, and he is close friends with Senhor Pereira, the owner of the Port."

"And the man in the painting above?" Owen asked.

"Teófilo Augusto Anselmo Pereira," Fernandes said. "A wealthy landowner near Vila Verde, now deceased. His family descended from *fidalgos*—in those days, a title somewhat like a knight. Today he would be like an English gentleman with no real title."

"So, is the other Senhor Pereira, his grandson? Miguel . . .."

"His great-grandson, senhora. Miguel Luis Alfaro Pereira."

"Those are mouthfuls of names," Owen observed. "What does the article say?"

"He is telling reporters that this bottle was a gift to his great-grandfather's ancestor in gratitude for some deed he had performed for the duke."

"What was the good deed?" Carla asked.

The detective's mouth drew to one side in what could almost pass for a smile, "He was vague about the deed. He only said this Port was a measure of the duke's gratitude to his family, and that he will never drink this Port, nor sell it. You see the puzzle, yes? Your pictures suggest Senhor Pereira no longer has it."

"Maybe he sold it after all," Owen said. "Even rich families can be hard up for money if their investments fail."

Detective Fernandes's eyes seemed to take on a deeper shade of blue. "Senhor Pereira did not sell it. I made a phone call to him last evening. A few weeks ago, Senhor Costa contacted him, wanting to sell a bottle of Port just like this to him. He had purchased it from someone else. He, too, remembered the newspaper article and wanted to sell it back to Senhor Pereira for a substantial amount of money."

Maria's earlier tale of card-cheating popped into Carla's thoughts.

"Senhor Pereira told him he must have a forgery. His bottle was still in his wine cellar."

"And was it?" Carla asked.

Again, the hint of a smile. "Apparently, there are two such bottles now—Senhor Pereira's in his cellar and Senhor Costa's that he wished to sell. One is a forgery, but which one? Senhor Pereira is having experts examine his own bottle."

Owen leaned forward with interest. "How will they be able to tell?"

The detective made circles in the air with his hand. "The cork's seal. The age of the paper and ink. They have their ways, and that is for them to work out. And now I have already told you much more than is usual when I am on a case." He gathered the two pages and put them back into his briefcase, then sat back in his chair, regarding Carla.

"At this moment, it is Senhorita Santos who interests me."

Carla felt blood rush to her face. "Senhorita Santos?" she said.

"When Chefe Esteves interviewed her, he did not feel she was telling him everything she knew. She told him she had seen no one except you and the thief whom you asked for help. But Senhora Gonzaga, the proprietress at the café across the street, saw another young man go in and come out again before you came along."

Maria's tearful face rose in Carla's mind. She felt reluctant to mention Paulo. For one thing, she would have to mention the trip to his apartment.

"Maybe it was just a customer who got scared when he went in and saw the broken case," she said. "The guy that stole the bottle from me probably stole the bottle in the case," she added, "and hit Senhor Costa over the head with it." Carla saw the corners of Fernandes's mouth twitch. Annoyed, she remembered his question at the police station as to whether she read mysteries.

"That's one possibility," he said after a pause. "Which reminds me . . . .." He pulled another paper from his briefcase and gave it to Carla. It was a photocopy of a mug shot showing a front view and profile of someone named Evaristo Marcelo Bernardino Serafim. Underneath the name, someone, probably Fernandes, had written in a tidy hand, "O Lobo."

"Is this your thief?" he asked.

For a moment, Carla had trouble breathing. She brought the paper closer, taking in the man's slicked-back hair, the scar on his lip, the other on his eyebrow. In her encounter with him, he had looked shifty and insolent. Some skinny little creep that got in fights. In the mug shot, his thin, hardened face looked predatory. "Yes," she said.

"He's been in prison before?" Owen asked. His arm went around Carla's waist.

"A robbery some years back in Lisbon. Recently he's connected with some black-market activity in Porto. And . . . more serious things." Fernandes shrugged. "Our concern, not yours."

"And now he's operating in Braga?" Carla willed herself not to be frightened. "O Lobo? Doesn't 'lobo' mean 'wolf?' In Spanish, it does."

"Ah, yes. Spanish is popular in California. And, yes, 'lobo' means 'wolf' in Portuguese, too. But . . ." he massaged his chin, ". . . getting back to Senhorita Santos, Chefe Esteves heard her offer to give you Portuguese lessons."

So Esteves was listening after all. "Should I have mentioned that?"

"We both want to take lessons," Owen said. "In fact, yesterday I told my wife to call her and set something up."

Deciding honesty was the best approach, Carla said, "I met with her this morning."

Fernandes nodded. "At a little after ten o'clock. At the Jardim de Santa Bárbara."

A feeling like ice water trickled down Carla's spine. "Excuse me?"

"You're having my wife followed?" Owen's voice rose. He sat back, his hands on his knees, his jaw jutting.

"And then you both went to an apartment building on Rua Jorge Araullo for some time," the detective continued to Carla. He steepled his fingers, his mouth a straight line.

Owen turned to Carla, his expression one big question mark.

"Maria was having boyfriend problems," Carla explained, wishing it weren't so complicated. She glared at Fernandes. Her shock had turned to burning anger and a sense of betrayal. She was being tailed, was she?

Fernandes's gaze sharpened. "What kind of problems?"

"Her boyfriend wouldn't answer her calls," Carla snapped. A protective instinct had kicked in where Maria was concerned, and she was loath to mention Paulo at all. Whatever his problems, she felt he wouldn't have killed Costa. The arrows all pointed to this O Lobo guy.

Fernandes tapped his fingertips together. "And you went with Senhorita Santos to his apartment because . . .?"

"I went for moral support. I felt sorry for her. He's giving her the brush-off. Haven't you ever been young and in love?" If she hoped to put Fernandes in his place, it didn't work.

"This isn't about me, senhora. It is about a young girl who is not telling the police what she knows. It is about a thief who is more dangerous than you think. It is about a serious forgery. And it is about my business to find out all the facts. Now. You didn't see Maria Santos before she came across the street to help you?"

"No," Carla said, her righteous indignation fading. "That was the first time I saw her."

"We feel she knows something important. Perhaps when you go for your language lessons, you can find out what that is."

"Why would she tell me anything?"

"A woman is more likely to confide in a woman. You already have her trust. She is confessing boyfriend problems. She may confide other things she might not tell the police."

78

Get her to tell me all and then report back to you? I don't think so. Carla already felt bad enough about the way Maria's visit to Paulo at her urging had turned out. Right then and there she decided to scrap language lessons with Maria and mind her own business. She folded her arms. "Detective Fernandes, I'm very sorry, but I would not be comfortable acting like a spy."

"You would be helping us to find her uncle's killer. Her life may be in danger as well."

"Oh!" Carla put a hand to her mouth. She hadn't thought of that.

"I don't want my wife in danger," Owen objected. "This is a police matter." To Carla he said, "We can probably get language lessons at International House."

"International House doesn't give Portuguese lessons," Fernandes said. "They teach other languages to native Portuguese speakers."

Looking flustered, Owen raised his palms. "Even so—"

"I understand your feelings, senhor, but your wife is already in danger. She can identify the thief who took a rare bottle from her yesterday. He knows that. There is much money involved. The sooner we know what Senhorita Santos knows about that bottle, the safer they both will be."

"It's too dangerous," Owen insisted. To Carla, he said, "I know we each make our own decisions, but please listen to me on this."

Carla's mind raced. The way Paulo kept urging Maria to stay away for her own safety meant he cared about her. O Lobo could be the "evil man" who visited him this morning. Maybe he had made threats about Maria. The key was to get Paulo to admit what *he* knew to the police. If she and Maria tried again, maybe together they could convince him, and the case could be wrapped up soon. She let out a wistful sigh. And then she could come and go as she pleased.

I'll do it," she said.

Owen looked at her in disbelief. "Carla!"

"Detective Fernandes is right. Maria might confide in me."

Owen got up and started pacing. He ran his hand through his hair. "We need to talk about this, Carla. I don't want you involved."

"I am involved, whether we want me to be or not. We can thank Senhor Costa for that," she added bitterly. If only she hadn't gone into his shop the first time. But then Maria would be facing whoever was out there all alone. Whoever killed him probably would have done so anyway, given the importance of that stupid bottle. *Both stupid bottles, the duke's and the three-thousand-euro bottle in the case.* Somehow, they were connected. But how?

"I'll call her tonight and ask for a language lesson tomorrow," she told Detective Fernandes, although it wasn't language lessons she planned to talk about.

He rose and picked up his briefcase. "Very good, senhora, I will be in touch. In the meantime, you each have my card. Call me if you learn something I should know."

"You'll have someone follow her to keep her safe, won't you," Owen asked anxiously.

"Sweetheart, have you forgotten?" Carla asked, and shot Fernandes what she hoped was a venomous look. "I'm already being followed."

"She'll be safe," the detective promised. They were at the door.

Owen looked from Carla to Fernandes. "I can't say I'm happy about this," he said.

The detective didn't reply. Instead, he held out his hand, and Owen gave it a grudging shake. Then, as if remembering his manners, Owen said courteously, "You're very fluent in English, Detective Fernandes."

"It is my business to be fluent. Crime crosses seas and borders. I am also fluent in Spanish, Italian, and French."

When the door closed behind him, Carla turned to Owen. "Don't be upset with me."   Owen pulled her close and kissed her forehead.

"I'm not upset. I'm worried."

"I'll have protection, so it should be all right." Despite her initial anger, now she felt a surge of relief that someone was following her. Carla shook her head then at the irony of her situation: Earlier today Maria had wanted her to spy on Paulo. Now Detective Fernandes wanted her to spy on Maria. Who else would she be spying on before this was over?

But Owen's kisses moved to her temple, then to her neck, and Carla decided to leave that question for later.

Chapter Nine - Carla Pays a Visit of Her Own

Morning came too early. If it were Sunday, Carla thought, stretching contentedly, they could laze in bed and revisit the night before. Instead it was shower, toast, coffee, and seeing Owen off at the door.

Once he had left for the hotel, still feeling like a purring cat from their amorous night, she reminded herself to call Maria.

"Olá, Carla," said Maria's listless voice.

"Maria, we need to meet this morning. It's about Paulo."

"No, I cannot. I have a class on Wednesday mornings."

Carla sucked her tongue against her teeth. She had assumed Maria's classes were always in the afternoon. "You'll have to miss it this once," she said. "A detective visited me yesterday. Someone else saw Paulo go into the shop."

She heard Maria's sharp intake of breath.

"And please get Paulo to come. He needs to tell us what kind of trouble he's in."

"I have tried to call him. I think when he sees my number, he doesn't answer."

"Give me his number, then, and I'll call him. Or you can go to his apartment again."

"He told me to stay away."

"Then let *me* convince him to go to the police. I'm sure they have his description. They'll be looking for him. It's better for him to go to them first." She wondered if she should tell Maria they'd been followed to Paulo's apartment yesterday. The police would be watching his door now, waiting for him to come out, waiting to see what the boyfriend looked like. It wouldn't be long before they realized Paulo was the one seen by the proprietress at the café.

When Maria didn't answer, Carla said, "Maria, I'm trying to help you. And help Paulo. If you won't meet with me and get Paulo to come, I'll have to tell the detective what you told me yesterday—that you saw Paulo go into the shop, too."

"You would do that!"

"I can't keep information from them without getting into trouble myself. And," Carla warned, "since someone else reported seeing him enter the shop, if you don't tell them what *you* saw, it will look like you're abetting him." Wondering just how extensive Maria's English was, she added, "Helping him. You could look like his accomplice, his partner."

After a pause, Maria said, "Where will we meet?"

"Museu da Imagem. On the second floor."

"They don't open until eleven."

"I know, but it's quiet and private, and no one will bother us there."

The Image Museum was easy for tourists to walk right by as they went through the stone arch of the Arco da Porta Nova on their way to Sé Catedral and shops further along on Rua do Souto. The red exterior looked like just one more colorful facade in a city full of them, even though it contained historical photos of the city and some beautiful photography exhibits. It was also free to the public.

"You'll be there, right?" Carla asked. "At eleven."

"Yes. I will try to have Paulo come too."

"You have to do more than try."

"I will do my best," Maria said in a flinty voice and hung up.

For a moment, Carla regretted coming on so strong. She could probably forget about any Portuguese lessons. Still, if neither of them showed at the museum, she really *would* call Detective Fernandes and tell him what little she knew.

There was a second reason she'd chosen the museum for their meeting: The name Gonzaga had stuck in Carla's mind. Since the museum didn't open until eleven, she'd have time to visit Senhora Gonzaga, the proprietress at the café across from Costa's wine shop.

There was a balmy feel to the air between Costa's shop and the Souvenir shop. Carla couldn't resist looking around, wondering if she could spot her assigned shadow. Was it the stooped old man across the street, fussing with his shoelace? Maybe he was just made up to look old, a Sherlock Holmes disguise. The man sitting in the blue Fiat parked not too far away from her? At first, it was comforting to set off, knowing she was being followed if any problems arose. Then a sense of resentment began to stir: Every move of hers would be known to the police, even though she hadn't done anything.

Better the police than O Lobo, kiddo.

When she reached the corner souvenir shop, she remembered the street bordering the other side of the building that helped to form its pie-wedge shape. The corridor she'd seen from Costa's office window could probably be entered from both streets. She walked around to check, nodding to herself when she saw the tall weathered door separating Costa's shop and an apartment building. Returning to the corner, she crossed to the café, sending a quick glance at the wine shop.

The white perimeter tape with POLÍCIA in dark blue letters made Carla wince. Poor Senhor Costa, whose only sins were cheating at cards and womanizing. How pleased he had seemed at the prospect of World Portal Inn's business! She turned back to the café.

The name, Hora do Café, was lettered high on the plate glass, in an arc. Below, the clear space was easily large enough for a person inside to see whatever was happening across the street. A small sign to one side posted the hours: 9:00 a.m. to 7:00 p.m., De segunda a sábado. *Monday through Saturday.*

A buzz of voices greeted her as she entered. She guessed the woman behind the register with salt-and-pepper hair pulled up in a knot must be Senhora Gonzaga. The woman's round cheeks, generous mouth, and plump shoulders suggested someone with no hard edges. She also cared about her looks: Her eyebrows were softly enhanced with a charcoal pencil. She'd used a pale lipstick, so that her make-up wasn't garish. Above her apron bib, a lavender scarf was knotted at her throat.

A long glass case to the right of the register displayed assorted pastries. A young, pretty girl in a green dress and yellow apron was just taking out two frigideiras—the delicious puff pastry meat pies Owen looked for whenever they went out for breakfast.

Three women at a nearby table were in animated conversation. One of them rested her hand on the handle of a baby stroller, rocking it back and forth. The toddler inside was a mass of pink ruffles, her sweet, snub-nosed face topped with black curls. She chewed on a pacifier, regarding Carla with dark, unblinking eyes. Carla felt a prick of yearning. How sweet it must be to choose baby clothes, to comb those curls. *Be patient, kiddo, it'll happen. It has to!*

At the next table, two young men watched the young waitress bring their frigideiras, halting their talk to give her admiring stares. Her dark hair was piled on top of her head. Her apron strings were pulled tight, emphasizing her small waist and full bosom. The men exchanged glances, and one muttered something as she set the plates next to their cafés.

At a corner table a thin young woman sat alone, texting. Carla grimaced, seeing the I-Heart-Braga tee, the sky-high, bleached-blonde ponytail. *An American tourist for sure.*

"You wish café, senhora?" the proprietress said, bringing Carla back to the purpose of her visit. The woman's shrewd eyes, at odds with her aura of softness, were sizing her up. To start off on a friendly foot, Carla asked, "What does the name on the window mean in English?"

The woman's gaze relaxed. "I think you would say, 'coffee break.' Maybe 'hour for coffee, or coffee time.'" She smiled, motioned toward an empty table by the window. "Sit, please," she said. In a louder voice, she called, "Rosa!"

Rosa looked over from the table where she'd been flirting with the men. Carla leaned close to the register. In a low voice, she said, "Actually, I would like to talk to you, Senhora Gonzaga, if you have a minute."

The woman gave Carla a sharp look. She took a small wrapped candy from her a pocket in her apron and began twisting the gold foil open. "You know my name?"

"If you have time, can we talk about . . . what happened Monday? To Senhor Costa?"

Senhora Gonzaga popped the unwrapped toffee in her mouth and sucked on it, the way Owen had sucked on sweets once when he tried to give up smoking. Something about the gold foil nagged at Carla.

She introduced herself to put the woman at ease. "I'm Carla Bass. Detective Fernandes came to my apartment yesterday." She'd found that, at least in business, a direct approach often elicited useful information.

"*Dete*tive Fernandes?" the woman asked around her candy, using the Portuguese appellation. "Ah. Sim. Yes. I remember you. A thief took your bottle."

Carla nodded. "Detetive Fernandes told me you saw what happened." She took pains to say his title right, since it felt as if Senhora Gonzaga had pointedly corrected her.

A sigh escaped the woman, one that sounded heavy with sorrow. "Sim. Yes." She motioned to Rosa, indicating she should take her place. "Come," the proprietress told Carla. "We talk outside."

On the sidewalk, near the door, Senhora Gonzaga stared across the cobbled street, lost in thought as she chewed the last of the sweet and swallowed it. "What you wish to know?"

"Was he a friend?" Carla asked softly.

"Yes. But that is not your question."

"No," Carla admitted. "I wanted to know more about what you saw before that man took my bottle." Technically it wasn't her bottle, she reminded herself, but Senhora Gonzaga wouldn't know that.

"Yes, I was here all morning. I see you take pictures of Senhor Costa's shop and go in and come out. I see you return, and I see the thief take your bottle and run away."

"What about in between? Detetive Fernandes said you saw another man."

"The chico." Senhora Gonzaga gave a dismissive shrug.

"Chico," Carla knew, was Portuguese for young man. "What did he look like, this chico?"

"He have curly hair, very dark. He was not tall. Maybe medium. Not too thin, but not fat. Young. Very nice face."

It could be almost any good-looking hunk in the area, not necessarily Paulo.

"He have a *covinha.*" Senhora Gonzaga tapped her chin. Carla frowned her puzzlement, and the proprietress twisted her fingertip deeper.

A dimple. Uh-oh.

Carla asked, "Was he in the shop long?"

"Sim." Senhora Gonzaga nodded firmly. "For some time. Maybe . . . quinze minutos. Fifteen minutes. Maybe twenty. Maybe half hour, even. We were busy in café." The proprietress spread her fingers and lifted her shoulders.

Despite all the maybes, the news jolted Carla. "Did you tell Detetive Fernandes how long he was inside?"

"Why you are so interested?"

The question caught Carla unaware. She thought quickly. "It was a shock, coming back and finding a dead body. I can't stop thinking about it. I keep wondering if I could have done anything to help."

Her answer apparently satisfied Senhora Gonzaga. "You could not do anything," she took a quick look at Carla's wedding band, "senhora." The proprietress dropped her voice and added confidentially, "That is not the only time this chico went into the shop. I see him go there maybe three or four times. And always Senhor Costa is upset after."

Fernandes was right. A woman *was* more likely to confide in another woman. "Was this over a long time?" Carla asked.

"Maybe one month. I think even more. Senhor Costa did not trust him. The chico was too much interested in special bottle in big case. So. Senhor Costa, he take it out of the case and put it away. He told me this." Senhora Gonzaga punctuated her statement with a firm nod.

"I see." Carla said. That had to be the bottle O Lobo grabbed from her. "Did Senhor Costa mention what he did with the bottle?" For a moment, Carla worried that she sounded too prying. But Senhora Gonzaga had warmed to her subject.

"No. He never talk about it again. But I see he is troubled, because, like I tell you, the chico comes back." Senhora Gonzaga wagged a disapproving finger in the air and leaned close.

"And I tell you one thing, between you and me, senhora," she said, running her tongue over her lower lip as if savoring the tidbit of information she was about to share. "That chico is up to no good with Senhor Costa's niece."

"They're seeing each other?" Carla made her voice innocent, wondering how much of this Senhora Gonzaga had shared with the police. *Paulo, you'd better come clean fast!*

"She have never told me anything, because we don't make conversation. She comes in here sometimes. But her uncle tells me she is student at the university. He was worry she is in love with that chico and will not finish her studies." Senhora Gonzaga folded her arms. "And I agree he is right to worry. A woman can recognize um mulherengo when she sees one, eh? A young girl cannot. Verdade?"

"Verdade," Carla agreed, trying to match Senhora Gonzaga's pronunciation. From the woman's expression, "mulherengo" must mean something like a playboy. Hoping to sound gossipy, Carla lowered her voice. "Do you think Senhor Costa ever talked to the chico about his niece? You know, tried to warn him off?"

Senhora Gonzaga shrugged again, the corners of her mouth turning down while she considered it. "No, I don't think so. Roberto . . . Senhor Costa would have told me. And I never ask." She half curled, half fluttered her fingers. "A good friend knows when to be silent."

Roberto. Carla filed that away. "His niece is the one who called the police for me," she said. "Lucky she was here."

Senhora Gonzaga nodded. "She comes into my café many times, sometimes with her books, and she studies, and then she goes to her uncle shop to talk. She has troubles, too, I think. Probably the chico, but I could not ask."

"No," Carla said, although she couldn't help thinking Senhor Costa might have been better off if Senhora Gonzaga had been a bit more meddlesome.

"Did the thief go into the shop before I came back?" she thought to ask.

Senhora Gonzaga shook her head. "No. No one else, senhora. Just the chico."

Carla gazed across the street to hide her amazement. Maria had said O Lobo went into the shop and ran back out.

How far would Maria go to protect her boyfriend? Even when he told her to stay away?

She turned to Senhora Gonzaga. "Maybe the thief who took my bottle went in and came out from the other side, and then came back to watch?" A memory flashed through her mind of O Lobo's thoughtful stare from across the street before he came over and pretended for five seconds to assist her. She thought of the door to the patio from Senhor Costa's office. "There's a side entrance to Senhor Costa's shop, right?"

Senhora Gonzaga gave her a long, considering look. "Is possible."

The atmosphere had changed. The woman's chilliness was almost tangible. Carla chastised herself inwardly. She had acted too snoopy. Asked too many questions. She must seem terribly insensitive to this woman. To bridge the growing discomfort, she said, "I suppose you'll be at the funeral. I'm sure it's hard. It's always hard to lose a good friend."

"The funeral is for family only." Senhora Gonzaga's voice was curt.

"I hope they find the man who did it," Carla said softly, wondering at the woman's changed demeanor. Maybe she was a lonely widow with a crush on Senhor Costa.

Or maybe plump, aging, sad-eyed Senhora Gonzaga was Costa's other woman.

Chapter Ten - A Sharper Focus

The Museu da Imagem was just outside the Arco da Porta Nova at the end of Rua dom Diego de Sousa. As Carla passed under the arch, church bells began striking eleven. She skirted the revolving postcard rack outside the gift shop next door and entered the free museum. With a quick smile for the young man at the desk, she walked past the metal spiral staircase that led to first floor offices. At the end of the long room, in the old stone tower, she took the elevator to the second floor.

So far, she was alone. She strolled around the current exhibit while she waited, her stiletto heels making soft, delicate clicks against the floor as her glance brushed over framed photographs of the Carnation Revolution lit from ceiling fixtures. Additional light filtered through pale curtains on the French doors that opened onto a small balcony above the entrance. A few weeks ago, Carla had persuaded the museum's director to unlock the doors and let her take pictures of the city's red-tiled roofs from the balcony.

She walked over, pinched a curtain to one side, and peered out. Paulo and Maria were coming through the arch, both dressed in jeans and tees. They couldn't have been far behind her. As she mulled over what to say, they disappeared from view, blocked by the balcony.

Then she spotted him, walking through the arch—the gaunt-faced man she'd seen go into Costa's shop Monday when she was photographing the exterior. There was no doubt it was the same man—high forehead, thin lips, wispy gray hair flat to his head. Boris Karloff in a worn, black suit. He stopped at the postcard rack.

The murmur of voices reached Carla from the elevator. She hadn't even heard it go down and come up again. She turned as Maria and Paulo stepped out, holding hands. *Clutching hands is more like it.* Maria face was anxious. Paulo's looked haggard, as if he hadn't slept.

"Bom dia," Carla told them, hoping her attempt at the Portuguese greeting would put them at ease.

They muttered their greetings and Maria tightened her hand on Paulo's, her mouth pinched. "What have you said to this detective?" she demanded.

"I haven't told him anything yet," Carla said, stiffening. *Don't get defensive; you're here to help,* she reminded herself. "He visited me and my husband to ask more questions, and he said he had a description of a young man who was seen going into your uncle's shop before I brought the bottle back."

"What you want with me? I have said I can tell you nothing," Paulo said. "And I cannot go to the police."

Carla made her gaze steady. "Since the police probably have your description, you should go to Detective Fernandes and tell him anything you know that can prove your innocence.

"And *you,*" she said to Maria," should go and explain that you were afraid to say anything Monday. Tell them you thought it over and convinced Paulo to come with you. Both of you will be seen in a much better light."

Paulo scowled. "You plan a lot of things for us, senhora. How do I know you are not the one who gives my description to this detective when he visits you?"

"I don't even know why I'm trying to help either one of you," Carla said. Furious, she turned and walked away, her steps sending a rat-a-tat-tat message.

An emotional interchange in Portuguese ensued as they followed her into the elevator. On the way down, they averted their eyes. Carla took a deep, calming breath. "Why can't you go to the police?" she asked Paulo.

He gave a rough laugh and looked away. The elevator stopped. Judging by his resolved expression as he stepped out, he wasn't going to volunteer anything else.

Keeping pace with him, she took out her camera, turned it on and showed him the picture of the duke's bottle. "Please, Paulo, what can you tell us about this bottle? I'm told you showed an interest in it and that you were seen going into the wine shop *many* times."

Paulo's face blanched. "You know about that bottle?"

"What!" Maria yanked his arm, forcing him to stop and look at her. Hurt and betrayal washed over her face. "You went into my uncle's shop many times? Why you never tell me!"

"Is complicated," Paulo said. He pulled away and kept moving.

"You know something about that bottle?" Maria persisted, following. "Why?"

"A man stole that bottle from me when I was trying to return it," Carla told him.

Paulo stopped abruptly. "What this man looks like?"

When Carla described her thief, Paulo said in almost a whisper, "O Lobo. Both of you must be careful. And stay away from me. Is dangerous for either of you to be with me."

"Remember, I have this." Maria reached down and patted her right boot at the ankle.

"Pah! That is nothing for someone like him. He is criminal." Paulo yanked the door open, then froze.

Carla followed him outside, curious. The man she'd nicknamed Boris Karloff was twirling the postcard rack, regarding Paulo. "Who is he?" she asked Paulo in a low voice.

Without answering, Paulo took off running. He sprinted across the street toward the beautifully landscaped triangle of Campo das Hortas with its velvety lawns, sculpted boxwoods, and sixteenth century stone fountain carved with grotesque animals. Narrowly missing a white Polo, he veered left onto Rua da Cruz de Pedra, then right, running past the Moreira house where tomorrow's auction was going to be held, and disappeared around the next corner.

The stranger stood watching, his lips quirked in what must be his grim version of a smile. With an almost courtly manner, he nodded to Carla, then to Maria, who had come outside; then he strolled back through the arch in the direction of Praça da República.

Carla rested her hand on Maria's shoulder. "Exactly what do you know about Paulo?"

Maria's mouth settled into an angry line. "Not very much, I think."

"Then you'd better go to the police before you're in as much trouble as he is. You'll be safer, too. This O Lobo really is dangerous," she said, remembering the mug shot and Fernandes's words the night before.

"Yes. All right. I will go."

"Do you want me to go with you?"

"No, I will do this alone." Maria rubbed her forehead. "But there is one thing I don't understand."

Carla smiled in spite of herself. "Only one thing?"

"Who told the police Paulo was in my uncle's shop?"

"Senhora Gonzaga." At Maria blank look, Carla said, "The proprietress of the café."

Maria looked even more puzzled. "She cannot have seen him. The chica, the girl, was at the register when Paulo went in and came out. Senhora Gonzaga is confused."

"Senhora Gonzaga must have seen him," Carla said. She almost mentioned her visit to the café, then decided to leave it as though Senhora Gonzaga had only talked to the police. "Paulo didn't deny going into your uncle's shop several times, did he?" she pointed out.

Maria swallowed as if her throat hurt. "Maybe *I* am confused. Maybe I only want that he was inside for a short time. Maybe she went back to the quarto de banho, the bathroom, and I didn't see her return. And then I was seeing that man, O Lobo, take your bottle." She pulled at a lock of her hair. "I don't know what to think."

"Tell the police the way you remember it," Carla advised. "It's their job to figure it out. But please call me after you've talked to them, okay?"

Maria nodded, her expression bitter.

Carla started to head toward the arch, then stopped. "What was that business in there about your boot?"

"Business?"

"You mentioned something in your boot and patted your ankle. When Paulo said—"

"Oh. That!" A weak smile flitted across Maria's face. "It is the knife I carry." She reached down, peeled back the hem of her jeans, and unclasped a small leather holster at her ankle, holding up a short knife with a thin blade.

"Very small, very thin, but it can, as you say, do the job." She held her hand out, clasping it tight, and twisted the blade back and forth as if skewering something.

Carla was speechless.

"My friend, Joaquim gives it to me, to make sure I am safe," Maria said as she sheathed it in the ankle holster and turned her cuff down again. "He is my neighbor in my village. He cares for me very much. He is probably better for me than Paulo, but . . .." Maria raised her palms.

Yeah, yeah, bad boys are more fun. Carla found her voice. "But Braga is supposed to be one of the safest cities. Why did he think you would need a knife?"

"It is a city, yes? My uncle is dead. You say the thief who took your bottle is dangerous. And Paulo fears two people. Joaquim gave me good advice, I think."

"Do you actually know how to use that thing?"

"Of course. I see my father do our matança do porco every fall."

"Matança do . . .?

"The pig-slaughter. This fall I will take you to see it."

"That's not necessary," Carla said quickly.

"Really, Carla, you must come. You will like it very much. We have a big feast afterward. My mother makes such good sausages. They collect the blood in a bowl—"

"From the slaughtered pig?" Carla closed her eyes, then opened them again, trying to shut out the vision of a pig spurting blood everywhere.

"Of course. And you will meet my family. Everybody has wonderful time."

The animation left Maria's face. "But now I must go and do, as you say, the right thing, and then go to class. I will call you tonight and tell you what the police say."

With a flutter of her fingers, she turned and walked in the direction Paulo had run, a slight lift in her step suggesting she might recover from heartbreak.

Carla stood at the door of the museum, lost in thought. Why was Paulo afraid of Boris Karloff's look-alike, when it was supposed to be O Lobo who frightened him? If Paulo had any sense, he'd run right over to the police station, since it seemed everyone was after him.

With a prick of guilt, she realized whoever was shadowing her would have seen Paulo with Maria. He could give his own description to Fernandes now—a description that would be close to Senhora Gonzaga's description. On the other hand, if the proprietress had been as informative with the police as she had with Carla, Fernandes would already know "the chico" was the boyfriend on Rua Jorge Araullo. *Fernandes was playing cat and mouse with me last night. It's only a matter of time before Paulo's picked up.*

At least Maria was on her way to the police station. Fernandes could thank her for that.

He won't.

Suddenly Carla felt tired of everything: Costa's death. Spying for Fernandes. Strange people popping out of nowhere. Stolen bottles. Thieves. Shadows. She checked her watch. Eleven forty-five. A good time to check out shoes, one of her more mundane pastimes, beckoning now with the promise of escape, if only temporary, from what felt like a steady drip of ominous unknowns.

Chapter Eleven – A Threatening Message

A few minutes later Carla stood under RCC Lux's red sign, admiring a stiletto-heeled sandal in the window. Black and turquoise straps crisscrossed over the instep. A turquoise strap went over the heel. She imagined a turquoise belt to pick up the color. Or a scarf, knotted at the throat. In Braga, scarves were easy to find.

Inside the store, the pretty sales clerk she'd talked to before was ringing up a sale at the register for an older woman. Carla was content to browse while she waited. She had always admired RCC Lux's decor—white walls, white display shelves, white floor, all working together to highlight colorful shoe displays. Someone had good decorating sense.

Three other pair of shoes appealed to her, including a pair of strawberry pink stilettos, but after trying them all on when the clerk was free, Carla settled on the turquoise and black and emerged from the shop with a light step. The walk home would be just enough to break them in. Her other shoes swung in the bag at her side.

To the left, two doors down on Rua de Janes, the aroma of coffee wafted from Café Faz Favor. *Mmm, good.* Carla walked over, sat at one of the outside glass-topped tables on the esplanade, and gave a harried waiter her order for a small espresso. As he rushed off, in spite of her earlier desire to forget recent events, the scene at the museum pulled at her.

Paulo. How is he involved in all this? He'd been seen at the wine shop, the scene of the crime. He'd been there before, too, without telling Maria. His visits had upset Senhor Costa, according to Senhora Gonzaga. And something he'd done made him frightened of more than one person.

Not your business, kiddo.

The waiter brought her espresso, and Carla took a grateful sip, savoring the gritty texture on her tongue, the velvety feel of it at the back of her throat. Between sips, she rotated her ankle, admiring the new sandal through the table's glass top.

Suddenly a shadow fell over her table, and a worn, black suit loomed at her side. Looking up and seeing Boris Karloff's doppelganger, Carla nearly choked.

He pulled out the gray, metal chair next to her as lightly as if it were made of cardboard and sat down. Even sitting, he conveyed an air of height. Carla put both feet on the ground, straightened her spine, and forced herself to give him a chilly look, despite the fact that his eyes were higher than hers.

"Yes?" she said in as cold a tone as she could muster.

"I have a message for your waiter friend," he said, startling her with a clipped, British accent edged by slightly rolled *r's.*

He poked his fingers in his breast pocket. Carla half expected him to pull out a small scroll with an edict. But no, it was an old-fashioned pocket watch. He wound it, tapped its glass face, regarded it a moment, then turned his attention on her, his bushy gray brows drawing together over a stare that made her fully appreciate the term "penetrating gaze."

"Tell him we want the bottle," he said. "The real one."

"I don't know what you're talking about." Carla gave what she hoped was a dismissive shrug.

"It seems there are more floating about," he said. "Tell him my employer wishes an explanation."

"Tell him yourself," Carla said, pretending her stomach wasn't doing flip-flops.

"He doesn't seem to want to talk to me."

Carla tapped her nails nervously on the table top. "Who are you, anyway?"

"Geoffrey Walsh. He'll know the name. Tell him we have figured out how he obtained it, and we want it back. And any other copies. Soon."

"Well, Mr. Walsh. I doubt I'll ever see him again."

"We haven't given his name to the police yet," Geoffrey Walsh continued, as if she hadn't said anything. "If he returns the bottle, or bottles, nothing will be said. If not—" Walsh smiled the terrible smile Carla remembered from outside the museum.

"I told you, I'll probably never see him again."

And the police probably already know who he is, duh.

"Otherwise," he said, "I will handle it my way."

His message delivered, he rose and held out his hand.

Carla folded her arms. "I don't shake hands with people who threaten me."

"The threat is for your waiter friend, not for you." He dropped his hand. "Tell him I mean business."

He turned and walked slowly away without a backward glance. Carla watched him continue up Rua Francisco Sanches, past the bright awnings and linden trees, his dark, retreating figure still managing to look sinister even from behind and from a distance. As soon as he turned the corner, she whipped out her cell phone and called Detective Fernandes.

He answered right away. "Yes, Senhora Bass?"

"I just had a visit from someone who seems dangerous."

"Where are you?"

She told him.

"Stay right there. I'm at the National Bank on Praça da República. I will be finished in five minutes. Sit outside where I can see you." He hung up before she could say anything.

"Okay," she told the silent phone and put it away. She looked around. What if Walsh came back? What if O Lobo showed up? Five minutes suddenly felt very long.

Where the heck was her shadow? She doubted he was the sweaty-faced, slightly obese man in the Hawaiian shirt at the next table, nursing a beer. Policemen didn't drink on the job, did they? But the beer bottle could be a front. What about the middle-aged man walking the German Shepherd? She hadn't noticed any dog before, though. Did undercover agents change props for different locations? Maybe her shadow was the bearlike man in khakis, polo shirt, and straw hat, eyeing the liquidation sign in the shop window next door. Or the younger, thirty-ish fellow on a skateboard who kept skating back and forth, first on one foot, then another.

She was debating whether to flag the waiter down for a second cup of coffee, when she spied Fernandes's dapper figure coming from Rua do Souto. Sunlight glinted off his glasses. He wore a light gray suit and was carrying his black leather briefcase. If she didn't know who he was, she'd think he was a businessman. He held his phone to his ear, nodding to his caller, said something, listened, and nodded again. He pocketed the phone as he came up to her and sat down in the chair Walsh had vacated. Setting his briefcase at his feet, he rested his elbow on the table and his chin on his fist.

Without so much as a "bom dia," he said in that quiet voice of his, "Tell me about your dangerous visitor."

Chapter Twelve - Carla Tells All and Learns a Few Things

"He said his name is Geoffrey Walsh." Carla described him, adding, "He's British."

Fernandes rubbed his chin, his expression hard to read. "Senhor Pereira's butler."

"Butler!"

"The family butler, as was his father before him, and his father before him."

"Was his father as scary-looking as he is?" Carla asked. "Like, did Pereira need therapy when he was growing up?" It was hard to tell if the tiny uplift to one side of Fernandes's mouth meant he was amused. That stone face probably worked well with criminals. "Shouldn't Walsh have more of a Portuguese accent by now?" she added.

"There are relatives in London, I understand. All his vacations are taken in England. And a few others of Pereira's staff are English."

"You know all that about him!"

"It is my job, senhora," Fernandes said patiently. He leaned back. "By the way, Chefe Esteves just called me. I understand you convinced Senhorita Santos to go to the station. She admits she saw her boyfriend, Paulo Sousa, go into the shop shortly before Senhor Costa died. Many thanks for your help."

"I tried to get Paulo to go, too, but Pereira's cheery butler scared him off."

"Start at the beginning, please."

Carla gave him an edited version of the morning's events, making it sound as if she had only just learned about Paulo's woes and evasions when she was in the museum, rather than when she and Maria went to his apartment.

"Those were Senhor Walsh's exact words? 'I will handle it my way?'" Fernandes squinted his eyes. "Senhor Walsh has no history of violence. No doubt he is bluffing, but . . . .." He ran a finger over his lower lip in thought.

Walsh's gaunt face loomed in Carla's mind. "He didn't sound like he was bluffing," she said. "The bottle Pereira has now is a fake, isn't it? And not the only fake, right?"

"There is no need for you to concern yourself with those questions," Fernandes murmured.

"Aw, c'mon, detective. Can't you tell me just that much? I've done everything you asked me to do."

Fernandes's pale blue eyes behind the wire frames appraised her. "When did I ask you to visit Senhora Gonzaga?"

She stared firmly back. "I wanted to find out exactly what Senhora Gonzaga saw so that I could compare stories." That was true enough. "I felt I could advise Maria better. She seems a little . . . naive." Carla tried not to think of the ankle knife in Maria's boot.

When he didn't reply, Carla said, "You have to admit, visiting Senhor Gonzaga helped me persuade Maria to go to the station."

"Yes. I suppose that was good thinking." Fernandes steepled his fingers.

"So, about the bottle . . . Walsh as much as said there were other fakes."

"You are a difficult woman."

I'll take that as a compliment. "How many fakes are there?" Carla asked.

With a tsk of annoyance, Fernandes said, "I will answer this one question, and then there will be no more questions, yes?"

"Yes."

"Yesterday the specialist to whom Senhor Pereira submitted his bottle confirmed it is a forgery. It was also the second such bottle they have examined. The first was from an agency acting on behalf of someone who remains anonymous. It, too, was a forgery."

"Wow. How long did it take to find that out?" At his frown, Carla said, "It's part of the same question."

"Senhor Pereira's man sent his bottle for inspection two weeks ago. I assume the other bottle was sent at a similar time."

"You knew all that when you visited us last night."

"Of course."

"And the bottle O Lobo stole from me *isn't* the second bottle the specialist examined."

"No. That wouldn't be possible."

"Two forgeries, and a third bottle everyone wants."

"Yes." Detective Fernandes tapped his fingertips together. "So," he murmured, but kept the rest of that thought to himself.

"O Lobo stole the bottle from me, but Walsh thinks Paulo has it," Carla said. "I wonder why he would think that. Senhor Walsh kept calling Paulo my 'waiter friend.' Maybe Paulo was a waiter at one of Pereira's parties, switched bottles, and took the real one."

"And how did Senhor Costa get the bottle?" Fernandes asked. His eyes turned a deeper blue. Was that a look of sincere interest? Challenge? Amusement?

"He probably won it in a card game," Carla said, and saw him startle to attention.

"You know about his scams?"

Scams? How interesting! "He was kind of a gambler," Carla said, hoping her own surprise didn't show. "Maria told me he tried to cheat at cards a long time ago to keep from losing an expensive bottle of wine. He got caught and had to pay up. If he tried that once, he'd try it again."

"It was more serious than occasionally cheating. Senhor Costa was what in America you call a *card shark*. He was a swindler in many ways. We have been investigating his financial records." Fernandes's voice turned brisk. "And now you know much more than you need to know, and I must be on my way." He rose.

Forged bottles. Swindling. Maybe even blackmail. Carla felt a rush of excitement, forgetting her earlier weariness of the whole matter. "Lots of people could want him dead," she said.

"That is for us to worry about. You have done your part. You have been of great help. Now you can go back to your interior decorating and your lessons in Portuguese."

"Wait!" Carla's enthusiasm wavered. "I still have a shadow, don't I? I mean, O Lobo is still running around loose."

"You will have a shadow until we solve this case," the detective told her, "but there is no need to involve yourself. We will close the case soon. Go back to your life."

He extended his hand. "Obrigado."

Just run along and play, now. I don't think so. Carla smiled her business smile, one she often practiced before meeting with a new client. She rose, too, and took his hand.

"I appreciate that, Detective Fernandes. I'm glad I could help."

The first thing she planned to do was track down Paulo and find out for sure why Pereira and his butler thought he knew where the duke's bottle was. Given how close-mouthed Fernandes was, he wasn't going to say anything more to anyone, not even to reporters. Look how non-informative the article in yesterday's paper had been: Costa's death, the broken glass case, the fact that a customer had discovered the body—everything else under wraps.

Detetive Fernandes glanced at her feet. "My wife likes shoes like that. They are very pretty. But, as I tell her..." He waved a forefinger. "...they are not much use if you have to run fast."

With that, he picked up his briefcase and walked away.

Chapter Thirteen - A Rude Surprise

Carla had always liked stilettos because they gave her height and brought her closer to eye level with clients, something she felt lent her more authority. Besides, Owen found them sexy. Now she eyed the black and turquoise straps ruefully. She supposed if she had to, she could take her shoes off and run. But how far would she get on bare feet, running along the square, sharp-edged cobbles paving so many of these streets?

Thanks for the spoiler, Fernandes!

A movement caught her eye from a far table—a man with his back to her, wearing a beige hoodie, which first struck her as strange, since the day had warmed up. Then it made sense—the undercover agent following her. He didn't want her to see his face. After Fernandes's parting remark, she was glad to know Mr. Shadow had her back, even if she wasn't supposed to see him.

Pretending she didn't, she gathered her purse and the bag with her other shoes, then hesitated. The events of the morning had left her feeling disheveled. What she needed was a cool wet paper towel against her face, a quick comb through her hair, and a fresh dab of lipstick. She went inside and made her way past crowded, glass-topped tables and the long gray metal bar, then turned down the dim hallway where the bathrooms were, taking a deliberate pleasure in the click-click of her new heels—*so there, Mr. Detetive Fernandes*—as she went inside the door marked "Mulheres."

When she came out again, she was suddenly thrust against the wall. A coarse hand clamped over her mouth. She found herself staring into the amber eyes of the man in the sweatshirt, his hood down now, revealing familiar slicked-back hair, the scarred eyebrow, the scarred lip. She tried to struggle, but for someone so slightly built, O Lobo was strong. His hand tightened on her mouth, his thumb gouging the muscle in her cheek so hard she winced in pain. He had maneuvered her so that the leg she stood on, the one bearing her weight, was pressed between his legs. There was no hope of trying to knee his groin. He gave a low laugh as if reading her mind. His other hand was at her throat, thumb and fingers squeezing on either side like a frightening caress.

"Do not make noise," he said in a low growl. "I squeeze hard, I can kill you." The pressure on either side of her throat increased. "It will look like you faint, and I am gone before you are found. You understand?" He took the other hand from her mouth and put it around her waist. With a smile, he said softly, "We look like lovers if someone comes."

"What do you want?" Carla whispered, mindful of his thumb and fingers still pressing on her throat.

"I see you talking to Paulo. I see you talking to the girl. To Senhor Walsh. And now that man in suit. What you are telling them?"

"They came to me," Carla managed to get out. "I just reported the bottle you stole. Monday afternoon. The police took me to the station."

"No, senhora. You were at the museum today with Paulo and the girl. You were with her yesterday at the Jardim de Santa Bárbara."

110

Carla felt her skin go icy. He had been watching? Where had he been each time? Why hadn't she seen him? Why hadn't her shadow?

"I warn you," he said. "Leave this alone, or I kill you. I know where you live. Beautiful garden in back." He gave a soft snort. "I know every way to enter a building."

Beyond O Lobo's shoulder, in the dim light of the hallway, Carla saw a tall outline, a shoulder; above that, the brim of a hat—someone hesitating, embarrassed perhaps to have stumbled onto someone's romantic moment on his way to the bathroom.

O Lobo said softly, "Promise to leave this alone, or I kill you right here. I just press harder, like this, eh? What you think, eh?"

The pressure increased. It was suddenly harder to breathe. Carla's mind raced wildly. He could kill her even if she did promise. Maybe he liked killing. Fernandes had said O Lobo was wanted in Porto for other things than theft. The man watching would think O Lobo's girlfriend fainted. While they sent for help, before finding out she was dead, he'd get away.

She couldn't knee him, but her left leg was free.

"What I think is that the man behind you won't believe we're lovers."

"Eh?"

For a split second the pressure at her throat relaxed. Carla guessed O Lobo was uncertain about whether to look over his shoulder. In that short instant, she lifted her free foot and stamped as hard as she could on his instep, giving him a hard shove and letting out a scream. With a howl of pain, O Lobo released her and toppled into the arms of the tall man who had closed the gap quickly.

What happened next was dreamlike. The man grabbed O Lobo's arms from behind in a movement so swift it must be professional, shoving him against the wall, yanking his wrists back and snapping handcuffs on his wrists in a smooth, continuous motion, while Carla leaned against the wall, taking in great gulps of air, watching. He was the bearlike man who had been looking at the liquidation sale in the shop window. In the way that fear makes the strangest details stand out, Carla noticed he'd managed to keep the straw hat on his head while subduing O Lobo, although now it tilted crookedly.

One hand holding O Lobo's cuffed wrists, he nodded to Carla and lifted the hat briefly with his free hand. "At your service."

O Lobo made a lunge forward, and the man released him so that O Lobo's weight sent him crashing to the floor, shouting and filling the air with curses. While he writhed on the floor, the stranger took a cell phone from his pocket, punched in numbers, and held it to his ear. As he spoke, Carla could only catch fragments, "...polícia . . . dois carros . . . Fernandes. . ." His call finished, he reached down and pulled O Lobo by the forearm to his feet, propped him against the wall, and quickly stepped aside as the man kicked at him and missed, nearly falling down again. After that, O Lobo leaned against the wall, staring sullenly into space.

Carla's screams had brought onlookers to the edge of the hallway. The bartender waved them back to their tables. Two matronly women at the forefront muttered to each other, sending furtive glances toward Carla, then her rescuer, then O Lobo, their hands gesticulating. Behind them, an elderly woman leaned on her cane, eyebrows lifted in disbelief. The undercover agent called something to them, and slowly they withdrew to the eating area.

O Lobo sent Carla a baleful glance. "Cabra!" he snarled.

The agent took his arm again in what was clearly an iron grip and shook it roughly. "Silêncio!" he warned.

To Carla, he said, "The police they come soon."

For what felt an eternity to Carla, the three waited in a silence broken only by the rise and fall of voices in the café. Carla's glance drifted to O Lobo's feet. One of his clean, white trainers that looked brand new had a dark mark where she had stamped. There was probably an angry bruise underneath, an idea that filled her with as much satisfaction as the two-note blares of police sirens now floating to her ears.

She took her new sandal off and examined the heel. Nothing had broken, she was glad to see, but her own heel felt sore. Small price to pay for being alive. She picked up the bag with her other shoes that she had dropped, along with her handbag. As soon as she got home she planned to go to bed and sleep forever, blot out this day.

Two of the officers who finally strode in turned out to be Chefe da Polícia Esteves and Agente Cunha. A third officer with light brown hair and a boyish face was accompanied by Fernandes. After greeting Carla politely in English, they listened attentively to the undercover agent's account in Portuguese of what had happened, looking from him to Carla with expressions of mingled amusement and respect.

As they all moved through the café to the entrance, Esteves and Cunha on either side of O Lobo, Carla tried to ignore curious stares from café tables. Outside, her shadow—

she probably never would learn his name—exchanged glances with Fernandes, inclined his head, then walked away. Esteves and Cunha led O Lobo to one of two police cars.

Fernandes said, "Senhora Bass, this is Agente Alcides." He indicated the younger policeman. "He can take you home."

"How did my shadow know O Lobo was in the café?" Carla asked. She shuddered to remember she had been so sure O Lobo in his hooded sweatshirt *was* her shadow.

"It seems he saw O Lobo sit down at a table outside just after I left," Fernandes told her. "He planned to call Esteves, but then you went inside and he saw O Lobo follow you." The detective nodded toward her feet, his mouth twitching ever so faintly. "I will tell my wife of your shoe maneuver."

Shoe maneuver. Carla tried to smile. *He has a sense of humor after all.*

"Although," he added gravely, "that only bought you time. If our man had not been here, perhaps you would not be so lucky."

If only he hadn't said that! Adrenaline shot through Carla, reviving the moment of O Lobo's hand over her mouth, the way he pushed her against the wall, the feel of his other hand on her throat, the malevolence in his voice, the cold fear she might die.

"Alcides can drive you home," Fernandes repeated, a look of concern on his face. "Or would you prefer I call your husband?"

"No, don't do that," Carla mumbled. Her voice sounded from far away. Her mind felt foggy. "He has meetings. It'll be hard for him to leave. I can tell him tonight what happened. Right now, I'd . . . I'd rather have a quiet walk alone." *No conversation. Just quietude.* She put her hand to her lips, as if to hold back the sour flavor in her mouth. O Lobo had seen her at the Jardim de Santa Bárbara, the museum; he knew her street, her building, the garden. *But the police have him. I'm safe.*

"I also will come this evening to talk with your husband," Fernandes said. "You have helped us catch a very bad man."

"He knew Walsh's name," Carla thought to say, coming out of her fog.

Fernandes looked unsurprised.

She rubbed the back of her neck where muscles had tightened, then let her fingers and thumb drift to her throat. Those were her carotid arteries O Lobo had been pressing. Weren't those the arteries that caused strokes when they were blocked? Even if he didn't press hard enough to kill her, she might have had a stroke. She felt cold again in spite of the early afternoon warmth.

"Senhora Bass?" The detective's voice roused her. She realized her hand was still resting against her throat. "You've had a shock," he said, gently. "Let Alcides take you home."

"Yes," she whispered. "Maybe that's a good idea after all."

Fernandes opened the passenger door, and Carla stepped inside. "Go home and rest," he urged. "You've earned it."

Chapter Fourteen – A Change in Plans

On the short ride home, a call came in on the dispatch radio. Alcides had a brief conversation in Portuguese, then lapsed into a silence Carla found soothing. Normally she would be tempted to ask polite questions—Do you have a family? Have you been with the police force many years? But now she appreciated the lack of talk. She stared numbly out the window. Her left cheek throbbed from O Lobo's gouging thumb. She probably had a bruise. And now her heel was throbbing, like an echo.

Alcides parked at the curb and came around to open her door, then walked her the few steps to her apartment. "I hope you take good rest, senhora," he said. He shuffled awkwardly, as if at a loss for what else to add. Maybe he'd used up his English vocabulary.

Carla held her hand out. "Thank you," she told him, adding, "Obrigada." She took her key from her purse and unlocked the door, willing her hand not to shake, then turned to wave at him as he pulled from the curb. Across the way, the barber, his hair a magnificent white mane matching his mustache, stood in his doorway, hands behind him, idly glancing up and down the street. *Probably waiting for customers.* He flashed her a curious smile, and she included him in her wave with some misgivings, wondering if being brought home in a police car would make her the subject of gossip with his clients.

She paused inside the small vestibule. Through the glass door onto the garden, branches of the Judas tree glowed with clusters of deep pink blossoms. The garden was so peaceful. She should make a sandwich and take it outside to eat. She could take her e-reader and sit in one of the wicker lounge chairs, reading and relaxing.

Halfway up the stairs, she pursed her lips. *On the other hand . . .*

Paulo didn't know O Lobo was in custody. Her curiosity revived, along with a new burst of energy. If he knew, would he go to the police and tell all? Should she tell him? She had gotten Maria to go to the station. And Fernandes had said a few minutes ago she'd helped catch a very bad man. If she got Paulo to turn himself in, even Fernandes would have to admit she wasn't a likely suspect anymore. *Wouldn't he?*

There was also George Walsh's threat to consider. Maybe the butler didn't have a history of violence, but there was a first time for everything. Look how freaked out Paulo had been at the sight of him. If she were in Paulo's shoes, she'd take her chances with the law. Meanwhile, O Lobo was on his way to jail. Her shadow's job with her was finished. Today, anyway. If she went to Paulo's apartment, Fernandes didn't have to know. And if she ran into that goony butler again, she could tell him she passed on his message.

True, she'd last seen Paulo sprinting along Rua da Cruz de Pedra, but that was before her chat with Walsh, her coffee with Fernandes, her tangle with O Lobo, her police escort home. Paulo could be home by now, in his yellow apartment, hiding out from the world. Unless he thought that O Lobo was staking out the apartment.

Who's going to tell him if I don't?

117

She retraced her steps, set the bag with her shoes on the bottom stair, opened the outside door, and peered out. No sign of policemen. The barber had gone inside his shop. She hesitated.

It's only a visit to let Paulo know. She set off slowly for Rua Jorge Araullo, limping to keep the weight light on her bruised heel.

Paulo's building and the shop next to it were as shabby as Carla remembered. She tried the buzzer for the outer door. *If there's no answer, I'll let it go. At least I'll have tried.*

The intercom crackled. Paulo's voice said, "Quem é?'

"Senhora Bass," she said. No answer. "Carla. Maria's friend," she added, when the pause lengthened.

The door handle finally buzzed, and Carla went into the dingy lobby. Now that she was alone, climbing the dimly-lit stairs, hearing her steps echo along the hallway and wincing from her bruised heel, she started to regret that an undercover agent *wasn't* following her. In her brief half-day of being tailed, she'd become used to the idea of invisible protection.

O Lobo is not looking for me, she reminded herself.

She knocked on Paulo's door.

He opened it slightly, and his unshaven face glared out. "What you want?"

"I brought you some good news, if you'll let me in."

Grudgingly, he opened the door wider.

Limping into the room, she glimpsed the sleeping area past the U-shaped counter. His bed was littered with clothes and an open duffel bag. The ashtray on the floor was full as before. *Thank you, Owen, for being just a four-a-day guy.* "Going somewhere?" she asked.

Paulo folded his arms. "What is the good news?"

"If you *are*, you're sure going to look guilty of whatever someone thinks you did."

"Why do you come here?"

"Look, Paulo, I know O Lobo has something on you and you're afraid of him, but he's been picked up by the police."

"How do you know this?"

You wouldn't dream how, buddy. To keep it simple, Carla said, "I was in the café where it happened. I saw him handcuffed and led away."

Several emotions chased themselves across Paulo's face, settling into relief, quickly replaced by desolation.

"You don't have to worry about him, anymore," Carla assured him.

He gave a bitter laugh. "Não. You are wrong, senhora." He palmed his forehead, and closed his eyes, as if to make some image go away.

"The police think O Lobo's connected with Senhor Costa's death," Carla said. "And they think that Costa's death is tied to the duke's bottle, the one I showed you on my camera, remember? Personally, I think O Lobo killed Costa, but you know something about that bottle, and you'd be smart to give the police any information you have." When Paulo shook his head, she added, "Otherwise, O Lobo will probably say *you* killed him."

Paulo's shoulders slumped. Wearily, he said, "Sit down, senhora." He indicated the green sofa in the lounge space. When she did, he sat in the padded chair next to it, absently pushing the sleeves of his tee to his elbows. He took

119

a pack from his shirt pocket and shook a cigarette out, then held the pack out to her. "You want?"

"No thanks."

"I cannot go to the police," he said, after he lit his. "I, too, am a criminal. I was not criminal before I meet O Lobo, but now I am. They will arrest me."

I, too, am a criminal? Carla swallowed nervously. Why had she been so sure he was just a victim? Still, he looked so vulnerable, so miserable, it was hard to feel afraid. *Well . . . very afraid.*

"Why don't you tell me about it," she said. She put her purse in her lap and folded her hands over it, leaning away from the smoke that drifted toward her.

"I stole that bottle the first time," he said. "Maybe five weeks ago. Six, maybe."

"The *first* time?"

"Is complicated, senhora."

"Call me Carla."

"I am saving my money to study to become a sommelier," he said. "You know what sommelier is?"

"Sure. A wine expert."

"There is society in America, in New York City, that gives certificate. I must go to New York to study. I know much about wine already," he said with a flicker of pride.

"Go on," Carla said.

"O Lobo comes to the restaurant where I work many times. He is supposed to be interested in his dinner, but he is studying me, I can tell. One evening he asks me do I want to do a small job and make a lot of money? From how he asks, it does not sound legal. At first, I say no. Then I think about it. It take long time to save money as waiter. I decide, if it is not drugs, I will do one job, no more."

"What did he want you to do?"

"To steal the bottle in your photograph. The one with the signature of a duke. To steal it from wealthy man who has mansion in the hills. During a party he gives."

Carla felt a thrill of vindication. Hadn't she said as much to Fernandes earlier? That Paulo, a waiter, might have stolen Pereira's bottle at a party? "Senhor Pereira," she said.

His eyes widened. "Sim," he said after a moment. 'Senhor Pereira is big shot here in Braga. He is giving an important party. Very big. Very grand." Paulo waved his cigarette. "He needs another waiter. The person who employs O Lobo wants me to go. I do not know this employer, but he has told O Lobo to find a waiter who knows wines. My job is to replace Senhor Pereira's bottle with forged bottle. O Lobo tells me where to find the real one in the wine cellar. When the butler sends me downstairs for more wine, I make the switch."

"And how did O Lobo know where to find the real one?"

"His employer knows. For some reason, he have been in the house, in the cellar."

"So you made the switch. Just like that!" Carla looked Paulo up and down, trying to imagine him in a white shirt and black pants, the uniform of waiters everywhere. Where would he stow the bottle? "How did you do it?" she asked. "Wouldn't there be a bulge in your shirt? In your pants pocket? Ah. The butler was in on this, so he looked the other way."

No wonder Walsh is so upset.

"Não. Não. The butler knows nothing about the plan. The man who gives O Lobo this job tells him where to find the bottle and O Lobo tells me and first gives me the forged bottle from where he hides outside the servant's door."

"So how did you manage it?" Carla pursued.

Paulo took a new puff, exhaling slowly. "I wrap forged bottle in towel, and walk with purpose as if to banquet table, but I go to cellar instead, where I make the change. I bring up three bottles from cellar, the special bottled wrapped in towel, and I walk with purpose again back to the kitchen. To look for better bottle opener, I say. I set two bottles on counter, the special one under my arm, still wrapped in towel. I look through drawers. I joke with waiters about this expensive house. When they go out with food, I take bottle to servant entrance and give to O Lobo, who waits in shadows. Then I open the other bottles and take back to main table. You see, if you do with confidence, there are no questions."

Paulo rubbed his bristly chin, his puppy eyes melancholy. "After O Lobo pays me, he asks do I want more jobs. I say, no, but he keeps asking."

"But how did Senhor Costa get the bottle?" Carla asked, astonished by the simplicity of the theft. "And why were you going into his shop so often?"

Paulo looked away. "Maybe a week later, by accident I go into the shop," he said after a moment. "I see the bottle next to another in the glass case. Both are so much expensive. I ask where he gets this bottle from—the one with the duke's name, not the other. He says it is long story. When O Lobo comes to the restaurant again, I ask him, 'Why do I steal a bottle for you only that you sell it to a man here in Braga?'"

"Did you mention the shop?"

Paulo nodded. "O Lobo is upset about this. Later he tells me his employer wants me to find out more. Is impossible for the bottle to be in Senhor Costa's shop, O

Lobo says, unless the forger is double-crossing. Maybe he sells the original and gives O Lobo's employer another forgery." Paulo rubbed his thumb and fingers together. "More money for the forger."

"Yeah, I get it," Carla said. The earlier conversation with Fernandes sprang to mind. Taking in Paulo's sad expression, it was easy to believe he was panicked by a situation expanding from one forgery to possibly two. Even three, if the bottle O Lobo grabbed from her turned out to be another forgery.

"And you don't know who Lobo's employer was?" she asked. "Or how he knew where to find the bottle in the cellar?"

He shook his head. "Is mystery man."

"Never mind," she said. "The police can probably find that out from calls on O Lobo's cell phone."

"O Lobo makes calls always from public telephones." Paulo ground his cigarette out in the ash tray.

Clever bastard. "So, then you started seeing Maria?" Fingering the strap of her purse, Carla knew instinctively she wasn't going to like the answer.

Paulo looked down, as if ashamed. "When I went back to ask about the bottle, it isn't in the case. I ask Senhor Costa, 'Where is your other fancy bottle?' I don't want him to know I understand what it is. I ask where does it come from, how does he get it? He tells me he bought it from a man in Galicia who bought it from someone in Porto. He laughs, then, and tells me he will make a lot of money. This I tell O Lobo." Paulo sighed. "I should not have."

"What about Maria?" Carla prodded.

"I go back to the shop again, and she is there. I hear her call him "tio," *uncle*. O Lobo tells me to accidentally meet her again in other places—he knows where she goes."

Of course, he does! Carla shivered, remembering O Lobo's recital of every place he had seen her.

"'Seduza a sobrinha,' he tells me," Paulo said. "'Find out from her where is the bottle is, or we tell police what you have done.'"

Seduce the niece. Even she could translate that. Carla frowned. "But wouldn't reporting you to the police get O Lobo in trouble, too?"

Paulo raised a palm, his mouth twisted in a jaded smile. "Senhora, I have so much cash if the police search here. Too much to put in bank with no explanation, because I am only waiter, yes? O Lobo can inform anonimato. How you say, 'anon . . . anoni . . .'"

"Anonymously?"

"Yes. And then disappear. I have no place to hide it. Unless I go away."

"Which would not be smart, Paulo. Especially now that O Lobo's in jail."

He massaged the lower part of his face. "Senhor Walsh remembers me."

"You're right about that." Carla gave him Walsh's message. "He says he hasn't given your name to the police yet. But O Lobo probably *will* finger you. And the police pretty much know where you are. If you go to the station and tell them what you just told me, I'm sure they'll be easier on you."

Paulo's only response was to hunch over, elbows on thighs, his thumbs and fingers forming parentheses at his temples.

"About Maria," Carla said, and the memory rose in her mind of Maria's surprised face Monday in the wine shop when she peered at the camera pictures showing her uncle had a bottle signed by a duke.

Paulo looked up.

"You never did ask her about the bottle, did you?"

"No. I can see very soon she knows nothing. I tell O Lobo this. And then I . . . just keep seeing her, because . . .." Paulo faded off.

Because you're in love with her.

"What about the other bottle?" Carla asked. Paulo looked puzzled. "The second one in the glass case. The 1812 bottle for three thousand euros? Someone stole that one, too. Do you think it was O Lobo?"

Paulo's lower lip jutted out, as he considered that. Then he shrugged. "No. I think he was only wanting the forgery bottle."

Someone wanted it, though.

She rose, aware all at once of how exhausted she was. And hungry. She'd eaten hardly any breakfast and no lunch. The image of a plate with bread, cheese, and some olives on the side rose in her mind, along with a nice crisp glass of vinho verde.

"I have to go. But please think about what I said."

Was he even listening?

At the door, she glanced back. He was still huddled over, face in his hands. She went out, closing the door quietly behind her.

125

Chapter Fifteen - Some Disconcerting News

Nibbling a cheese sandwich at the kitchen counter, Carla realized she hadn't stopped by the antiques store to tell Senhor Godinho she wanted the mirror. She finished her sandwich and dialed the shop, letting him know she'd stop by the next morning to pay for the mirror. The auctioneer would arrange to have it picked up for shipping along with the two paintings she expected to snag tomorrow night. With Mrs. Demming's generous budget, it was hard to believe she wouldn't outbid any others.

After hanging up, she went into her office and briefly reviewed information she'd researched about the artwork. Mrs. Demming liked the Barbizon school of painting and had been excited when Carla told her two landscapes by António Carvalho da Silva Porto were coming up for auction. Mrs. Demming was getting more enthused about Portuguese artists and antiques each time Carla contacted her, and Silva Porto from Portugal was one of the greatest naturalist painters of the 19th century.

Satisfied everything was in order, Carla ran a hot bath and let herself luxuriate in the suds, feeling remnants of the day's tension drain away. She wrapped herself in her terry robe, noting in the bathroom mirror the red mark on her left cheek. How badly would it bruise? When she rubbed it gently, it didn't particularly hurt, but the back of her jaw ached from where O Lobo had pressed his thumb. In the kitchen she poured a glass of Alvarinho. Forgoing the garden, she took it to the bedroom, which overlooked the garden anyway. Outside the window, clouds of pink blossoms on the Judas tree stirred from a slight breeze. Setting her glass on the night table, she plumped several pillows, then curled up on the bed, and turned on her e-reader.

She flipped through her stored books and came to one of Rhys Bowen's Molly Murphy mysteries set in the last century, *City of Darkness and Light.* She'd already read it, but suddenly 1903 Paris seemed an appealing escape from bottle thieves and present-day dead bodies.

After two chapters, she drowsed off into a deep, dream-filled slumber. Molly's maid was muttering about shoes. Carla was running barefoot down a New York alley with O Lobo chasing her. He was gaining on her. Carla tried to run faster. She couldn't. She tried to wake up, but the syrupy tide of the dream kept pulling her back to see how it ended, despite a feeling of dread.

Finally, she wrenched herself out of the dream. Relief pulsed through her, seeing the familiar print on the wall of Bom Jesus do Monte, the Baroque hillside cathedral with its zigzagging "five senses stairway" climbing up, up, and up. She pressed her hands against the bedspread, reassured by the smooth fabric under her fingers. As she lay groggily awake, trying to shake free of the dream, she became aware of cooking aromas. Hot olive oil. Paprika. Fish.

She clambered out of bed, still feeling woozy. Barefoot, she limped into the kitchen, where Owen, wrapped in his chef's apron, dropped a new piece of battered fish into a pot of hot oil. A platter on the counter was heaped with golden strips of fried potatoes.

He grinned. "Awake? You must have had quite a day."

"You wouldn't believe what kind of a day!"

His grin faded. "What happened to your cheek?"

"Long story. Just take care of that fish while I get dressed. I'm starving." She limped out of the kitchen and down the hall to their bedroom and changed into slacks and a light tunic.

Over dinner, she told him everything that had happened.

Halfway through her account, Owen put his fork down, visibly jarred, his gray eyes wide. "Jeez, Carla! You were supposed to be in safe hands. Fernandes said there was nothing to worry about."

"I *was* in safe hands. My shadow came spectacularly to the rescue," she said lightly, hoping to calm him. "You'd have been impressed."

"You could have been killed if he hadn't been in time."

"I'm here," she pointed out.

"What about this weird butler giving you messages for Paulo? And I don't like the sound of Paulo," Owen added. He ran a hand over his face as if to brush away a swarm of worries.

"Paulo made a stupid mistake, and that's for him to explain to the police. Or to Senhor Boris Karloff, now that I've passed on his message."

"What were you thinking, Carla? Going to Paulo's apartment? Alone? If anything happened, no one would know where you were."

"I think you're overreacting. I had my cell phone." Carla brushed away her earlier unease when she was in

Paulo's stairwell, before he let her in and she heard his story. "Now that he knows he's safe from O Lobo, he'll probably . . ."

But Owen wasn't listening. He picked up a French fry, dipped it in tomato sauce, and put it down again, his brow still puckered in concern. "Promise me you won't do something like that again. Don't you realize how much you mean to me? Can you even imagine how I'd feel if—"

Carla had never seen him so upset. "I promise," she said in a small voice.

"*Seriously.*"

"Seriously. Cross my heart." Carla did a little crisscross over her heart with her finger. "But getting back to O Lobo," she said, "Fernandes said I helped catch a very bad man."

Immediately, from the look on Owen's face, she quickly added, "Meanwhile, I've invented what Fernandes calls my 'shoe maneuver.' I hope O Lobo's foot is a mess."

Owen managed a weak smile. "Nice to know you have dual-purpose shoes. Nobody messes with Carla." The light tone Owen attempted didn't match his face.

"Not if they want to walk again. *Mwahaha.*"

"What matters is that you're safe," he said. "Promise me you'll let the police tie this up and just stick to finding more antiques for your rich client."

"Don't worry! I've had enough excitement to last me a lifetime."

"Toast?" Owen raised his glass.

"Toast." They clinked.

"The fish came out well," Carla said. "Moist and succulent."

He turned his palms up. "Chef's specialty and your favorite—bacalhau."

"The potatoes are crispy too."

"What can I say?"

As she took the next bite of fried cod, Carla's thoughts made a sudden U-turn back to Geoffrey Walsh.

It was all very well for Detective Fernandes to dismiss Walsh's threat as bluffing. But what if the butler *wasn't* one to make idle threats? What if he really had decided to handle Costa *his* way? Walsh was a tall man. An angry shove could have sent Costa sprawling to his death. No one had mentioned seeing a tall creepy man on the scene near the time of death. But there was that outside corridor between the wine shop and the souvenir shop. He could have returned to the shop from the other street. *No. Because he'd have to have a key to the gate. But maybe he could pick locks. And Walsh didn't know Costa had given me the bottle. But what about the lump on Costa's forehead? Well, he could have done that with the bottle from the case, after Costa fell.*

"What?" Owen said, his worried frown returning.

"What do you mean, what?"

"You squinted your eyes."

"I'm reading a Molly Murphy mystery," Carla said. "It has a complicated plot." She speared a new bite of cod and concentrated on her plate.

Since Owen had cooked, Carla took care of the dishes, over his protests that she should rest and relax with a book after her harrowing day.

"Uh-uh," she said. "When I cook, you wash up, and vice versa. That's our routine," she reminded him. "Go out on the balcony and have your smoke in peace."

Besides, she found it more soothing to perform a normal task like rinsing plates and table ware. Trying to rest and relax with a book hadn't worked. She had just finished loading the dishwasher and pressing start, when the outside buzzer gave its distinctive blat, announcing a visitor outside the entryway.

After a few minutes, they opened the apartment door, and Detetive Fernandes nodded his greeting, looking dapper and solemn as ever. He sat in the overstuffed chair, they sat on the sofa, and without much preamble, the detective gave Owen his own recap of events.

"We found the bottle O Lobo took from your wife in his apartment," he added. "He was keeping it for someone. At present, he will not say who, but . . ." Fernandes made his circle-in-the-air gesture with his hand, ". . . it is only a matter of time."

"Do you think it's a forgery?" Owen asked.

"We are sending it to the expert who examined the other bottles. In another week or two we will know if it is authentic. If so, we will return it to Senhor Pereira. If not . . .." The corners of his mouth turned down. Clearly police business.

Owen squeezed Carla's shoulder. "Sounds like things are pretty much wrapped up, babe. O Lobo's picked up. They have the bottle. We can celebrate with a trip to Ponte de Lima this weekend."

"I regret to say things are not wrapped up," the detetive said.

In the silence that followed, the evening's fish and chips did a tango in Carla's stomach. Maybe Fernandes was having the same second thoughts about Geoffrey Walsh that had occurred to her. They had O Lobo. They had the bottle.

But did they know who ordered the theft from Pereira? And who had the second forgery examined by experts? She couldn't imagine the butler would have orchestrated the bottle switch for reasons of his own, but she was sticking with her earlier insight that he could have killed Costa in a fit of rage.

And there's still the other bottle that was in the case. Maybe he snatched it for Pereira.

Before she could ask anything, Fernandes said, "It is the matter of Paulo Sousa that concerns us."

"Why?" Carla asked, the word coming out scratchy and breathless. "Hasn't Paulo . . . Sousa contacted you yet?"

"No."

That was disappointing news. But then, Paulo hadn't made any promises.

"I visited his apartment this afternoon," she said, and saw Fernandes transform from a low-key, close-to-the-vest investigator to an ice sculpture. The warmth in the room turned wintry. His stare grew colder as she struggled through her rationale. "I suggested to him that things might go better for him if he comes forward on his own, now that he didn't have to fear O Lobo."

"They would," Fernandes said, "if his story were true. But O Lobo says they have been friends for many years. According to him, they have done many jobs together, and Sousa was eager to do this one."

"I don't believe that," Carla exclaimed. Hadn't she warned Paulo that O Lobo would put the blame on him? "O Lobo's lying!"

"Possibly. But we cannot discount his information. At present, we consider Sousa dangerous. You should not have gone to his apartment," Fernandes said, his pale eyes still chilly. "I remember telling you to concern yourself with your decorating business and not with this case."

Carla's face turned hot. *Your decorating business! Your fluffy little occupation!*

Owen leaned forward, his elbows on his knees. "Shouldn't you guys have picked him up for questioning by now?"

"And what about the other bottle?" Carla asked. "The one that was stolen from the case?"

"Eventually we will bring Sousa in for questions," Fernandes told Owen. "But at present we may learn more from surveillance."

He turned his gaze on Carla. "As for the Maoel Beleza de Andrade, we have our own ideas where to find it. And I would advise you to stay away from Sousa. You may only have been lucky because he feels you are on his side." He stood, the purpose of his visit apparently concluded.

After he left, Carla leaned against Owen, glad of his arms around her waist. With the detective's departure, her defensiveness was replaced by doubt. How could she have been so misled about Paulo? "I probably *shouldn't* have gone to Paulo's apartment," she admitted in a muffled voice.

"No, you shouldn't have." Owen tightened his arms. "I keep telling you, that curiosity of yours—"

Carla drew away. "It wasn't curiosity," she tried to explain. "I was trying to help him."

"I'll bet anything you also wanted to find out whatever you could."

This was so true that, guiltily, Carla could think of no reply.

"Do you have to go to that auction tomorrow night?" Owen asked, changing the subject.

"Of course I do! I'm bidding on two paintings for Mrs. Demming. It's my *job* to go! It's my *business*." Carla could hear her own querulousness.

Owen put a palm out. "Okay. Okay."

The troubled look on his face gave Carla a new pang of guilt. "Sorry," she said. "I guess my nerves are catching up with me."

"Don't mind me if I worry," Owen said softly. "Just the same, I'm going with you."

"I'm glad," Carla said. This was her first evening auction, and she had planned to take a cab rather than drive through the rabbit warren of turns that kept cars off the main pedestrianized areas. Now they could walk home together, maybe stop at Café Vianna and enjoy the lights from the fountain on the square. She snuggled her head against his chest. They stood that way for a quiet moment.

"By the way," he said, "Maria called while you were asleep. She wanted you to know she'll be busy the rest of this week. Her cousins are flying in from New York and Miami for the funeral Friday. They'll be with her aunt, and her parents are coming for a few days. We can start language lessons on Tuesday evening. I think that's the whole message. She suggested Monday, but I told her you have Skype meetings on Mondays."

"Language lessons?" Her head still cradled against his chest, Carla ran that through her mind. Maria hadn't washed her hands of language lessons after all.

That thought was followed by another: She should probably warn Maria that Detetive Fernandes considered Paulo dangerous. Carla chewed her lip.

How, exactly, did one start a conversation like that?

134

Chapter Sixteen - A New Friend

At breakfast, Carla decided against calling Maria. After the argument in Museu da Imagem, it wasn't likely she'd contact Paulo soon. Even if she did, she was probably safe. Carla brushed aside her initial opinion that Paulo was dumping Maria. He was in love with Maria. He was trying to protect her from O Lobo when he warned her to stay away. Her safety mattered to him.

Buttering a piece of toast and watching Owen sip his cafezinho, Carla kept her thoughts private. After he left for the hotel, she made her usual second cup and stood at the French windows, mulling over O Lobo's claims that he and Paulo had worked together before.

Liar! O Lobo had a calculating mind. He had crossed the street Monday, pretending to help, and then snatched the duke's bottle from her. He had followed her into the café yesterday, threatening to kill her. He exuded nothing but menace. Paulo exuded despair.

As for scary Mr. Walsh, maybe Fernandes was right that the butler had no history of violence, but Walsh and his employer wanted the duke's bottle as much as O Lobo and *his* employer did. Either one of them, Walsh or O Lobo, could have entered Costa's shop through the passageway between buildings.

So, how can someone get in if they don't have a key to one of the gates? If it were O Lobo, he'd know how to pick

135

locks for sure. But a dignified English butler with a heritage of serving the Pereira family? Maybe. Maybe not.

Ah! The souvenir shop opened onto the same corridor, she reminded herself. Say the shop owner went to check on back stock. Walsh could walk in and go right through to the outside space, then go into Costa's office. Costa probably didn't keep his office door locked during business hours. He wouldn't need to if the street gates were locked. "Walk with purpose," Paulo had said. Most of the customers in the souvenir shop would be tourists. They'd think Walsh worked there if they even noticed him walking out onto the corridor.

And how would he get away again, unseen, carrying a three-thousand-euro bottle of rare Port from the smashed case? He'd return through the souvenir shop. In the wine shop, he could put the bottle in a bag and wait for the right moment to stroll through the gift shop again, this time looking like a tourist.

Carla nodded. *It could work.* Fernandes's scolding and her promise to Owen hummed in her mind like mosquitoes. She shooed them away. It was worth a little visit to the souvenir shop to see how easy it was to get into the corridor. Maybe O Lobo had paid Paulo a hefty sum to steal the duke's bottle, but Paulo didn't seem like the murderous type. She might find an overlooked clue that could keep him from going to prison for a murder he didn't commit.

The police are thorough, but they see what they want to see.

She was about to take her cup into the kitchen, when Natália Freitas came out on her balcony across the way and took a cigarette pack from a pocket in her flowered apron. She tapped out a cigarette, lit it, the metallic lighter flashing in the morning sun, and inhaled with such obvious satisfaction Carla could almost feel it. Then she leaned one elbow on the ornate scrollwork of the wrought-iron rail. Spying Carla, she waved with her cigarette.

On impulse, Carla set her cup on the dining table, opened the French windows and stepped out. "Would you like a cafezinho?" she called. "I grind the beans myself."

"Nice! I will come!"

"Finish your smoke," Carla called, seeing Natália glance at her cigarette. "That'll give me time to make a new pot."

In the kitchen, Carla measured sugar and fresh water into a saucepan and let them come to a boil while she ground new coffee beans. She had just put the grounds into the pot and removed it from the burner when a blat from the intercom announced her neighbor's arrival. Carla buzzed her in and waited at the apartment door as Natália came up the stairs holding a loaf wrapped in a dishtowel. It was the first time Carla had seen her without an apron, and she had to admire the woman's taste: black capris, white three-quarter-sleeved blouse, red wedge sandals. Her bright red fingernails matched her bright red toenail polish. *Stylish!*

"Bem-vinda," Carla said, hoping she'd pronounced the word for welcome right. "It's nice to get a chance to know you."

"I have brought some bread," Natália said. "You like broa?"

"I *love* broa! Come on into the kitchen."

In the kitchen, Natália unwrapped the loaf and sliced it with the serrated knife Carla gave her, placing slabs on a plate, while Carla poured scalding coffee through the filter into small ceramic cups and brought them to the table. They slathered butter on the dense, yeasty cornbread, sipping their cafezinhos. In no time at all, despite language hitches, Carla felt she had made a friend. An older friend, true—maybe forty-five—but Natália's red shoes and nails said she had lots of spirit. She and her husband, Manuel, the barber, had two married daughters. One lived in Porto and one in Lisbon, which Natália called *Lisboa.*

"You have been to Lisboa?" she asked. At Carla's head shake, she lifted her hands as if incredulous. "You must go! Is beautiful city. Is birthplace of Fado. You have heard Fado?"

"I've heard *of* it. I haven't heard it."

"Não! I will do something about that. I have CDs. You have player, yes? I will bring you some. Let's see . . . You must hear Amália first. The greatest fadista." Natália finished her slice of bread and buttered a second piece. "But I do all the talking. Now you must tell me about yourself."

She listened as if entranced while Carla explained her interior design business and Owen's role as coordinator of the hotel renovation for the hotel chain start-up.

"But why he comes to Portugal? Why not a big city in America?"

"His employer already has a small chain in California," Carla explained. "He wants to start an international chain, and he's starting with Portugal because his heritage is Portuguese. A grandmother or great-grandmother, I can't remember which."

Natália pursed her lips, considering it. "Why Braga?"

"He wanted a big city, but not as big as Porto or Lisbon . . . *Lisboa,*" Carla corrected. "Braga has a unique charm. Especially in the historic center."

"Yes, Braga has much charm," Natália agreed, then sighed. "Is exciting time for you both," Natália said. "My job is not so exciting. But I like it much."

"What do you do?"

"I am bookkeeper three days each week at Casa Stop. Is very nice shop with things for your home. Towels. Yarn. Aprons. Thread." Natália moved her hands in the air like an orchestra conductor. "A little of everything."

Carla smiled. "I'll have to stop by one day and look for an apron. What days do you work there?"

"Monday, Wednesday, and Friday. But you will not see me. I am always in office in back room. But . . ." Natália shrugged, "is perfect job for me. I have time for myself and for Manuel. I can come home for lunch. On days I don't work, I watch my programs." She leaned forward. "RTP2 is good station. They have music programs and telenovas. SIC also has."

"Telenovelas?" Carla asked. The word sounded like television novels.

"Like your soap operas," Natália said. "Manuel complains I watch too much, but he always reads newspaper after he close shop." Natália waved a shiny red fingernail at Carla. "You should watch. Is good way to learn Portuguese. I see you have learn some words already."

"I don't think I have time," Carla hedged. Soap operas had never appealed to her. To change the subject, she said, "You must miss your daughters."

Natália sighed. "I miss Catarina too much, yes. Lisboa is so far away. I am lucky Porto is close. I can see Fátima and Miguel and our grandson more often." A pensive look came over her face and she fell silent.

Just when Carla was thinking they had run out of conversation, Natália cleared her throat. "Something I am wondering," she said, then stopped, as if embarrassed to ask.

"Yes?" Carla stiffened, expecting to field questions about children—*How many you have? You don't have? Is problem?*

Instead, Natália said, "Yesterday Manuel see policeman drive you home. Everything is all right?" Natália's brown eyes welled with concern.

Carla quickly swallowed the last sip of her coffee, then traced the cup's ceramic rim with a finger, studying the dregs of her coffee.

Natália said, "I should not ask about such a thing." After only a slight pause, she added, "But you know? Sometimes is good to talk to someone."

Carla nodded slowly. Bethany was an ocean and a continent away; it was hard to have heart-to-hearts on Skype; their talk on Mondays and Fridays had become mainly biz talk. She could hardly unload to Maria. Too young, and too much a wild card. Owen would worry all over again if she tried to discuss her latest thoughts with him. Besides, even though he never complained about his work, Carla could tell he had his own pressures at the hotel.

"Maybe is too personal, I am sorry to ask," Natália said. Her voice was subdued, apologetic, while the radar of her curiosity pulsated in the air.

"It's a long story," Carla told her. "Are you in a hurry? Would you like another cafezinho?"

"Yes. Please." Natália propped her elbows on the table and rested her chin on the backs of her interlaced fingers.

Carla poured two new cups and put them in the microwave. When they were ready, she brought them to the table.

Taking a deep breath, she said, "Monday I found a wine-seller dead in his shop.'

"So! *You* are who finds the body! The owner of Adega do Costa! I read in the newspaper."

"Yeah, well there's a lot the article didn't mention," Carla said, and everything came pouring out.

Natália's brown eyes had grown wider and wider. "Mãe de Deus!" she said, when Carla got to O Lobo's mugging in the café hallway. She fumbled in her slacks pockets and brought out her pack of cigarettes, then promptly shoved it back.

"That's okay," Carla said. "We can go out on the balcony."

On the balcony, she finished her story.

"So that is why the purple on your cheek."

"Does it show again? I thought I did a good job of covering it with make-up."

"Just a leetle. But I wonder about it earlier." Natália lit another cigarette and peered at Carla's black and turquoise stilettos around a curling wisp of smoke. "These are the shoes?"

"They are."

Natália regarded them a moment, took another puff, and then made a tsk-ing sound. "Is sad this O Lobo get Maria's chico in so much trouble."

Carla glanced over in surprise. For a mother with two daughters, Natália seemed a bit laid back about Paulo's foibles. "Do you know Paulo?"

"I do not. Still. He is young. He has make mistake. He stealed a bottle. This is bad. But I don't think he is killer."

"I don't either," Carla said, relieved to hear Natália express her own thoughts. "Detetive Fernandes and my husband both think I'm naïve. From what I've seen of Paulo, though, he's just a mixed-up guy who made a dumb decision."

Natália nodded. "Yes. Is unfair. We must help him."

"Excuse me?"

"We must find who killed Senhor Costa."

Carla looked away, covering her mouth with her palm to hide her smile. *I have a sleuth partner?* Turning to Natália, she asked, "Who do you think did it?"

"Maybe this O Lobo person. Or maybe this person who hires O Lobo."

"His employer. Yes," Carla said. "But why?"

"Because he thinks Senhor Costa, how you say, double-cross him?"

"I didn't think of Costa double-crossing him." *But if he cheated people, why wouldn't he double-cross them if he had the chance?*

"How to be sure?" Natália mused.

Carla eyed her neighbor thoughtfully. Maybe Natália just wanted to help a guy down on his luck. Maybe she fancied herself in the middle of a soap opera. A telenovela about star-crossed lovers. Or maybe Natália had a morbid interest in how crime stories in the newspaper played out. What did she really know about Natália?

She decided to go with the I-just-want-to-help-poor-Paulo scenario. "There's an outdoor corridor between Senhor Costa's store and the corner souvenir shop," she told Natália. "It has gates opening onto two different streets. I'm thinking of trying to enter it from inside the souvenir shop." She saw her neighbor's eyes light with interest.

Natália had reached the end of the cigarette. Looking around, she spied Owen's ashtray on the marble-topped table and ground out the stub, giving Carla a perplexed look. "I don't see you smoke."

"My husband's the smoker."

"Is not good, I know," Natália shook her head. "Someday I give it up." In a more energetic tone, suggesting that idea was history, she said, "When do you go to this place? I can come with you."

Carla hesitated. She leaned against the balcony's wrought iron rail, idly observing a silver Polo parked half on the curb below. Did she want a sleuth partner? The past few days had been part nightmare, part adventure, horrible but oddly exciting, with an edge of unreality that must come from being on her own in a foreign country.

On the other hand—Carla glanced at Natália, who was consulting her wristwatch—*I speak no Portuguese. I'll have a better chance getting into that corridor with someone who knows the language.* "Maybe an hour from now," she told her neighbor. "First I have to take care of some business at an antique shop."

Natália's face fell. "I cannot go so soon. Today I make Manuel a special lunch. And tonight we go out to dinner. Is our anniversary."

"We can go this afternoon," Carla said, warming, now, to the idea of an ally who could help her poke around Costa's building. "Maybe two o'clock?" she suggested. "We could meet in front of the souvenir shop."

"Two-thirty, is better."

"Two-thirty, then," Carla agreed, and they went back inside.

Patting Carla's arm, Natália said, "You make good cafezinho. If you like, one day I show you how to make broa."

"I would love that! I've been trying some Portuguese recipes, but broa looks complicated."

"Is nothing." Natália flicked the air with her hand.

At the door, Carla thought to say, "Happy Anniversary, I hope your Manuel takes you someplace special."

"We are going to Restaurante Centurium."

"Good choice!" Restaurante Centurium belonged to the elegant Hotel Bracara Augusta, a hotel with a Roman theme, including pillars at the entrance from the lobby into the restaurant, and an ancient, historic well inside the restaurant.

After closing the door, Carla limped back to the kitchen to do a quick wash-up. She had thought of wearing flats today, but, strangely, the stilettos were more comfortable, once she had cut portions of a dish towel and made a folded pad to put under her left heel.

Just walk slowly.

The day looked newly promising as she gathered her purse, put her camera and cell phone inside, and set off for the antique store.

Chapter Seventeen – An Expedition

At Antiguidades do Minho, Carla found the owner on a rickety chair at the back of the store cleaning an oil painting with bread crumbs. He rotated the wad of bread gently, his knobby knuckles bulging from arthritis. The gilt on the wide, ornate frame was chipped, but Carla could see that a beautiful cityscape underlay the grime.

He propped the painting against another chair, his smile turning his face into a web of wrinkles. "Your mirror is wrapped up and ready for your person from Porto. When do they come?"

"Saturday, when they pick up the paintings from tonight's auction," Carla said, as they walked to the front of the store, the proprietor's wiry torso swaying from side to side above his bowed legs.

After she paid him, there was time for a bite of lunch before meeting Natália. She walked quickly to Tasquinha Dom Ferreira, a traditional family style restaurant a few doors away, and ordered sardinhas fritas com arroz de feijão—fried sardines and rice with beans. While she waited for her order, Carla took a small notebook from her handbag and pen to sketch out her imagined layout of the souvenir shop. She hadn't been inside, but since the entrance was at the sharp corner, the door to the outside corridor had to be in the longer wall opposite. The corridor was probably a holding area for deliveries and a place for garbage cans that would be put on the street for later pick-up. She hadn't really noticed when she glanced out Costa's office window.

Carla tried to picture herself browsing around the souvenir shop, sidling over to the door, asking innocently, "Where does this lead?" Or maybe Natália could ask in Portuguese. Either way, though, what was their excuse for wanting to go into the corridor? She doubted they could just walk through the shop the way her imagined culprit would.

The question still pricked at her as she walked along Rua Dos Chãos to the shop where Natália was waiting outside the open door. A small sign in the window read Loja de Presentes de Torres.

Natália had added a gauzy, red-flowered scarf, looped in casual swirls around her neck. Her dark eyes shone with anticipation. "We are ready, yes?"

"We need a plan." Carla glanced at the café across from Costa's shop, remembering that Senhora Gonzaga seemed to notice a lot of what went on. She sidled closer to the open doorway to stay out of sight, and peered inside the souvenir shop.

Inside, at a counter against the side wall to the right, the proprietor, tall and angular with a long, thin face was showing a fold-out collection of postcards to a young, cherubic-looking man in Bermudas. Behind the owner, a door led to what must be the shop's inventory. Directly across from Carla, light poured through the glass pane of a door exactly where she had sketched it. So far, her idea was feasible.

"Maybe you could look around the shop while I buy postcards," Carla said to Natália in a low voice. "Or ask the owner about something you don't see in the shop, so that he has to go to back and check."

146

"I have better idea," Natália said. "I will explain you are American reporter. You are writing report for magazine about shops in Braga. Many buildings here have much history. You want to write the history of his shop."

Carla gave her a thumbs-up. "That's great!" She took out her notebook, turning the page with her sketch. "I do write about Braga on my blog. Tell him I want to interview him."

"He will like magazine better than blog. It sounds more famous."

Carla shook her head. "Then I'll have to make up a phony magazine name, and he'd want to see the article. This way, I can give him my card and write a post he really can read—if he knows English and if he's online. With a shop, though, he should be," she added. Still, Costa hadn't had a website for his shop. Not one she could find, anyway. But the idea of writing about Loja de Presentes de Torres appealed to her. Why *not* a post about a quaint souvenir shop? With a pang, she remembered she had wanted to write about Costa's wine shop before she found him dead behind his counter.

"Okay," Natália said amiably. "I tell him you have famous blog people read all over the world."

Hold that happy thought, kiddo.

They entered as the cherubic-looking customer left. The owner gave them a wide smile, showing nicotine-stained teeth. Carla drifted around the shop while Natália engaged him in conversation. The usual tourist items littered display shelves and racks: statues of the Sé Catedral, scarves, baskets, ashtrays, thimbles, ceramic roosters, bookmarks, calendars with scenes of Braga. A woman with dark, rippled hair gazed at a display of refrigerator magnets. A twenty-something guy

147

twirled a rack with maps and guidebooks. A man with a cigar fingered a ceramic mug showing a picture of a rooster.

Carla jotted down perfunctory notes to include in an introductory paragraph, then focused on the shop's arched ceiling, weathered stone walls, angled corners, and tiled floors. The architecture would matter more than souvenirs to potential clients interested in classical lines and old-world charm.

While she was considering taking a photograph of the bronze, hand-shaped doorknob on the door to the corridor, the proprietor came around his counter with Natália, who said, "Senhor Torres is happy you will write about his shop."

There was a stir of interest from the other customers, then they went back to perusing merchandise.

"I speak some English," Senhor Torres told Carla. Looking around proudly, he said, "This is the oldest shop in Braga."

Perfect! "How old is it?" she asked. Aided by Natália's translations, Carla took notes, as Senhor Torres expanded into the shop's history, including the large inscribed stone in the side wall that had been taken from ruins of the older city's castle wall.

"There are many such stones in buildings all over our city."

After writing this down, Carla let her glance drift to the door in the far wall. "Does that go outside?" she asked, hoping she sounded curious and not merely stupid, since clearly it did.

He nodded. "Go outside and take a look. I must . . .." he nodded at the man with the cigar who had taken the ceramic mug to the counter.

She and Natália went out onto the rectangular patio. Garbage bags propped neatly against Torres's wall and stacked boxes from a recent delivery confirmed her earlier guess. Across from her, Senhor Costa's wall, painted the same bright blue of the tiles in the front façade, was bare of bags or boxes. A rose bush in a pot to one side of the office door was unfurling white petals, and dark pink geraniums bloomed in a pot on the other side.

So Senhor Costa liked flowers. For some reason that brought a sting to Carla's eyes. She blinked it away, took her camera from her purse, and began snapping pictures—Senhor Torres's wall, the green-framed doorway to his shop, the street gates at each end. Near the gate at one end, two wrought-iron chairs flanked a glass-topped table.

She moved to Costa's doorway and window, hoping Senhor Torres wouldn't wonder, if he came out, at her change of subject matter. Natália had stooped to daintily pick up something with her fingernails from the threshold of Costa's door. She wrapped it in a handkerchief and put in her purse, flaring her eyes at Carla like someone from a spy movie.

Carla walked over and peered in Costa's window. The office looked much as she remembered it—magazines and envelopes were still in tidy stacks on his rectangular desk. The computer was gone, though, along with the folder stuffed with papers. The police must have taken them to headquarters to examine at leisure. His door to the wine cellar was closed, as was the door to the store. An empty room with no clues that she could discern.

At least she knew her suspicions about one thing were true. The corridor was easily accessible.

Senhor Torres's reflection appeared behind her in the window pane, like a shimmery ghost, the corners of his mouth turned down. "The owner was my friend," he said quietly. "Someone killed him for expensive bottle of Port. The police say the case was smashed to pieces."

Carla turned, taking in the pouches under Torres's eyes, his slumped shoulders. For a moment, she thought of telling him she had found the body, then decided it would make her story about a blog post too coincidental. Instead, she asked, "Did you see anything when it happened? Hear anything?"

"I didn't see or hear nothing until the police came. And then so many customers came in to ask what has happened, because the street is closed. I couldn't tell them nothing." He shook his head. "I had to read the newspaper the next day."

For a man who spoke "some English," Senhor Torres was pretty fluent. "It must be terrible to lose a friend that way," Carla said.

"Yes," he murmured. He waved a finger toward the table and chairs by the gate. "In the evening, we would close our shops and sit there and have glass of Port and talk before I went home. My friend had too many worries."

Too many worries? Carla regarded the chairs, then adjusted the wrist strap on her camera. As if only idly interested, she asked, "What kind of worries?"

"He wanted to leave Braga. He wanted to go to Brazil, but he could not."

Wow, that's a new wrinkle. Carla made her voice incredulous. "Who would want to leave a beautiful city like Braga?"

Natália had composed her face into an expression of polite interest, but her posture signaled high alert.

Senhor Torres gave Carla a warm smile. "I am glad you like our city." He sighed, then. "My friend wanted to get away from things. Many things."

Like O Lobo and Walsh hunting him down for the duke's bottle, maybe?

Senhor Torres cupped his hands around his elbows and rocked back on his heels. "'Francisco,' he told me many times, 'Francisco, I could disappear in Brazil, but for my niece. My sister depend on me that I watch over her. I cannot go nowhere.'"

"Por que o Brasil?" Natália asked. "Brazil is dangerous country," she told Carla.

Senhor Torres cocked his head. "Ele tinha um monte de dinheiro." He rubbed his fingers and thumb together. To Carla he said, "You see, he had very much money. You can live well in Brazil with money. And Brazil is very big. If you change your name, no one can find you."

"Why did he want to disappear?" *Why did he want to change his name?*

"He have . . . *had* . . . bad relation with his wife."

What a wonderful gossip Senhor Torres was! This was more than Carla had hoped for. She wondered if he had shared any of this with the police.

"I tell him, 'Go, Roberto! Go to Brazil. I will look after your niece.' But he say to me, 'No, it is more than look after her. I have to keep money for her to finish her university program.' You see, the niece is very smart student," Torres explained, "and this is her first year."

A flurry of questions rose in Carla's mind, all of them questions she couldn't ask: *How much money? Money from gambling? Black market? Blackmail? Did he ever mention Paulo?*

151

Natália, like a hound on the scent, said in a voice that dripped sympathy, "Seria solitário a desaparecer sozinhos . . .." To Carla she explained, "It would be lonely to disappear all alone."

Senhor Torres's lip curled in a confidential smile. "My friend would not be all alone. You see . . .," He opened his palms as if to lay out a scenario for them, but a woman's high, clear voice called from inside the shop, "Hello? Hello! Anybody here?"

Senhor Torres dropped his hands. "Perdoe-me." He indicated the door with a jerk of his head, his face conveying his disappointment at not finishing his story, then motioned them to follow him inside, where two elderly women waited at the counter. The earlier customers were gone.

Carla gave Senhor Torres her card, underlining her website with her fingernail. "You can read my blog post about your shop next week."

Outside, she took a picture of the shop's entrance. Inside, Senhor Torres was behind the counter again, leaning forward, his elbows propped on it as he showed her card to the two women.

Natália said, "We can go to that café and talk."

Senhora Gonzaga's café? I don't think so. "The owner is the woman I told you about," Carla said. "I don't think we should be talking about Senhor Costa under her nose."

"Under her nose?"

"We shouldn't talk about him in front of her. I think she had a thing for him," Carla said.

"Excuse me, can you help me?" The thin American woman Carla had seen Tuesday in Gonzaga's café came up beside them. She smiled apologetically and waved what Carla recognized as a map of historic Braga. Today she wore blue boyfriend jeans, a coral tee and silver flats. A small camera hung from a strap around her neck.

What horrible sunglasses! They were enormous and round, with wide, white plastic frames.

"Can you tell me where the Bis . . . the Bis-cainhos museum is?" the woman asked, then grimaced. "I'm probably saying it all wrong."

"You said it well," Natália offered kindly, but even Carla could tell she hadn't.

"Go across Praça República," Carla said, "then turn right on Rua do Souto. Then keep going, and just past the arch take another right. You can't miss it."

"You're from the States!" The woman folded her map, put it in her pocket, and rested her hand on her hip, her expression chatty. "So am I! Nevada. Reno. Tiffany Hill." She held out her hand to Carla.

On a different afternoon, Carla would have enjoyed pursuing this conversation, but right now she wanted only to discuss the patio area between the two shops and Costa's desire to go to Brazil. She gave Tiffany's hand a brief press, then said, "You might want to hurry. They close at five-thirty, and there's a lot to see."

"Oh." Tiffany looked disappointed. "Okay."

"Especially the gardens," Carla added, to soften her brush-off. "They really are amazing."

"I *love* gardens! Thanks for the tip."

As they watched her hurry off, Natália asked, "What is 'have a thing for'? You say the woman in the café have a thing for Senhor Costa."

"I think she liked him a lot. More than a friend would," Carla said. "She got strange when I asked questions

153

about him. Let's go to Jardim de Santa Bárbara to talk. It'll be private enough."

A few minutes later, they sat among the hedges and rosebushes. The sun brightened the yellow and purple pansies, not far from where she had sat with Maria Tuesday morning under her shadow's surveillance, while somehow O Lobo had spied on them.

Carla said, "So, what did we find out?"

"Senhora Costa have much money." Natália held up one finger. "He want to disappear in Brazil." Two fingers.

"Running off with a lot of money could explain why someone wanted to kill him. And why he'd want to disappear," Carla said slowly. *Money from con jobs? Wine fraud?*

"And he would not be alone," Natália said, holding up three fingers.

Carla nodded. "Maria said he had another woman." She wondered again whether Senhora Gonzaga was that very woman. Either way, maybe he planned to dump both her *and* his wife and run off with some young chick.

"Is like a telenovela."

"Yeah," Carla said absently. *Who, exactly, did he want to disappear from?*

"I find a clue," Natália said. "A candy wrapper." She opened her purse and took out a lacy handkerchief. Unfolding it, she showed Carla a shiny gold candy wrapper. "Is evidence."

"I think Senhor Costa had a sweet tooth," Carla said. "I found one like that Monday in his office." She drew in a sharp breath, remembering her trip to the café on Tuesday. Like a replay of a video scene on her smart phone, she saw again Senhora Gonzaga pull a toffee from her pocket, open the gold foil, and pop the candy in her mouth.

A gold foil wrapping just like this one.

"Manuel, he likes candy, too. Most when he worry about something," Natália said. "I think it relax him to unwrap it. He is telling himself, 'be calm.' When I see him unwrap candy, slow and careful, I say, 'Come, Manuel. Tell me what is worry you.'"

"Costa certainly had lots to be worried about," Carla remarked, her thoughts running in all directions. *Senhora Gonzaga killed Costa! And then returned recently to check for loose ends. Not a smart killer, though, leaving candy wrappers around.* Carla rubbed her forehead. *Maybe Torres left it and it isn't connected at all to Costa's death.* But she hadn't noticed Torres eating candies. His teeth indicated he was a heavy smoker.

It could be just a candy wrapper, left by Costa when he came out to water his flowers. Maybe Costa did *have a sweet tooth.*

"This woman at the café you say likes him." Natália said. "He would talk to her. Maybe she knows things about him, and that is why she don't like you to ask questions. She protects his memory."

Yeah, right! Although . . . Natália might have a point. Did Senhora Gonzaga know Costa was a card shark and was dealing in possible wine fraud? Did she know he was trying to sell the duke's bottle back to Pereira? She had acted as if she only knew Maria's "chico" was interested in the bottle, but that could be an act. Her coolness at Carla's questioning could, as Natália said, to protect Costa's memory. *Or his crimes.* Whether friend or lover, Senhora Gonzaga might be the loyal type. *And maybe that's why she killed him? But,*

155

then, how does Walsh, O Lobo, and O Lobo's employer figure into this new scenario? Carla sighed.

"Is complicated case, yes?" Natália said, regarding the wrapper with a mixture of pride and happiness. "Here." She handed Carla her handkerchief. "For your detetive friend," she said, using the Portuguese appellation.

Carla had a sudden flash of Fernandes's disapproving face as she tried to explain why she was giving him a toffee wrapper found in the corridor outside Costa's office door. How to explain what she was even doing outside Costa's office door. *He's only told me to butt out of this case how many times?*

Natália would want to know what Fernandes said when she gave the wrapper to him. For a moment, Carla contemplated tossing the wrapper and telling Natália she'd somehow lost it. But then, she'd have to lose the handkerchief as well. *And the wrapper might really be a clue.*

"I'll return your handkerchief later," she said glumly. She put it inside her handbag. "I guess we should go."

"Yes, because I have hair appointment. I must look nice tonight."

"I'm still trying out hair salons," said Carla as they rose. "Yours does a nice job."

"I go to Andréa on Rua Dos Chãos. She is very popular," Natália said. I get you her card."

At the garden's edge, she paused and, in a low, confidential voice that made Carla lean closer, said, "I must tell you something."

"Yes?"

"I have told Manuel we are shopping. I don't mention we are looking for how a killer gets into a shop. He should not know this, or he will worry too much."

"I won't say a word," Carla promised. Then, "Owen's the same way."

"These men, eh? They think we are so fragile and they must protect us. Although," a girlish smile flitted across Natália's face, "sometimes that is nice."

Chapter Eighteen – Dinner at A Taberna do Félix

Félix Taberna was conveniently located near the house where the auction was to take place. On Largo da Praça Velha, not far from Arco do Porto Novo, it was one of Carla and Owen's favorite restaurants. Gray lace overlays on white tablecloths gave a touch of romantic elegance. Soft lighting on vintage photographs and an old typewriter on a cabinet, lent a contrasting atmosphere of nostalgia. They decided to eat outside since the evening was mild.

The owner, Guilhermina, brought them each a small glass of white Port while they consulted the menu. After they clinked glasses, Carla studied Owen's abstracted face. He had seemed lost in thought at the apartment when she told him about meeting Natália. He hadn't been particularly chatty as they walked to the restaurant.

"Lots of meetings today?" she asked.

He swirled the Port in his glass for a moment before answering. "Just small stuff. The fellow I mentioned who applied for night clerk? The one from Germany who could speak English and Portuguese as well as German? He's decided to go to a hotel in Lisbon instead."

"You have several languages covered for daytime," Carla reminded him. To make the point that World Portal Inns was unique and catered to a world clientele, Owen had planned for two daytime desk clerks, one who could speak

English, Spanish, and Portuguese, and one who could speak French, German, and Portuguese. "You said the brochures will be in five languages," she added. "Someone who checks in at night can read those and talk to one of the daytime clerks if they have questions."

A young waitress, new to them, brought them a basket of bread and took their order.

"Gabriela wants to expand the lounge to include a special library," Owen said after she departed. "A library lounge." He frowned. "I don't know." Gabriela Coelho was the main decorator from Rocha Conceitos Interiores, the interior design company revamping the hotel decor. "She wants to stock it with Spanish and Italian books, as well as German, English, French, and Portuguese," he said tiredly. "Even more languages, if possible."

"That's a great twist," Carla said, as the waitress brought their wine, a crisp Alvarinho to go with the fish they'd ordered. Usually she didn't care for Gabriela's ideas. Her color choices for instance—mauve and ivory walls, gray drapes patterned in black and silver. Elegant, yes, but not as inviting and warm as peach and earth tones might have been.

Now, thinking of how she missed access to print books in English, Carla said, "Guests would appreciate a lounge like that. You should add Asian languages, too. You're going to get tourists from everywhere, you know."

"They're on vacation, Carla. They're sightseeing. Besides, where do we stop? Russian? Bulgarian? Hungarian? Swahili? Urdu?"

"Why not? It'll take a lot of books if she wants to call it a library lounge. You could have dictionaries, travel books, some fiction, a famous poet or two. A library like that sends a statement. It *is* World Portal Inns, after all. And they can't be sightseeing every single minute."

"That's pretty much what Gabriela said."

"Two women can't be wrong," Carla quipped. "She'll have to start ordering books soon, though, to have it stocked by September. Then again, if you start small, you can have art pieces on the shelves here and there. Clients would love it."

A young couple wheeled a baby-stroller across the cobbled plaza toward Anjo Verde, the vegetarian restaurant next door. Carla eyed them wistfully, hearing the soft, cooing tone of the mother's voice as they went into the restaurant. That was something Carla appreciated about the Portuguese: They took their children with them everywhere. Family was everything.

She took a quick sip of her wine. *One day.*

Owen furrowed his brow, immersed in hotel business. "Plumbing's still in a state of disarray, to put it mildly. Bathroom fixtures, new connections to the main line . . .." He ran a hand through his hair.

Their food came, Bacalhau com Broa. For a few moments, they ate and sipped quietly. The sun had drifted to the horizon. The sky was turning to that inky blue that made street lamps and windows seem more golden. A warm breeze stirred the air.

"You look nice," Owen said softly, his eyes resting on the lacy front of her dress.

Carla rested her fingers lightly on the back of his hand. The waitress placed a globe with a candle on their table. As its flickering glow sent patterns of light and shadow across Owen's face, Carla was reminded of their first date seven years ago.

His employer had hired her to choose art for the rooms of a new branch in San Jose, one with an English Country theme. She'd picked Gainsborough and Constable prints. Owen had come to see the selections, and the spark between them had been there from the first, although they didn't date until the project was finished. Like tonight, they had eaten at an outside table, soft lamplight gilding the space around them as the sky faded into night.

She pressed her wine glass to her cheek, remembering. Seven years of twilit dinners with candle flames casting their glow coalesced into a single instant. A wave of contentment washed through her. Despite all that had happened lately, it felt good to be here, half a world away from the cacophony of Bay Area rush hours, enjoying dinner on a breeze-touched evening, under stars, in Portugal. For tonight she could forget dead bodies and a thug who had tried to kill her. *And maybe a murderous café owner.*

Her contentment wavered. She hadn't thought to take the candy wrapper—Senhora Gonzaga's candy wrapper, as she now thought of it—from her handbag when she changed clothes for the auction. The crinkly paper lay in the bottom of her purse coddled in Natália's handkerchief. Carla could imagine it beaming questions at her: *When are you going to tell Fernandes? What, exactly, are you going to say?*

"Tiago's still looking for a bartender," Owen remarked, as he cut a small chunk of cod.

"Too bad Paulo is in so much trouble," Carla said. "He wants to be a sommelier. Wanted to be," she amended.

Owen's hand paused. "How do you know that he wants to be a sommelier?"

"He told me. He said that's why he switched the bottles when O Lobo offered him the job. He wanted to go to some school in New York, and he thought he couldn't save enough money on his waiter's wages."

Owen forked the bite of cod along with a piece of potato and chewed slowly. When he swallowed, he said, "I know it sounded to you as if Paulo was pouring his heart out, babe. You have pillow written all over you, which is why people confide in you. They want to put their head on your shoulder."

Carla rested an elbow on the table and palmed her chin. "But?"

"But he was probably giving you a sob story he worked out for you to pass along to the police. You heard Detective Fernandes say O Lobo and Paulo worked together before. And that Paulo's dangerous."

"O Lobo *claimed* they've worked together," Carla corrected. "But Paulo isn't the violent type, Owen. Trust me. He's scared of O Lobo."

"Uh-huh."

Carla bristled. "I'm not as gullible as you seem to think!" She brushed a few breadcrumbs that had fallen on the tablecloth into a neat little clump near the corner, then tapped her fingernails against the table edge. "I do have good intuition about people, you know."

"I'm not saying you don't, babe. I'm just saying you're too soft-hearted."

"Be glad of that," Carla teased. "That's why I overlook all your foibles. How's the landscaping coming along?" she asked, when the worried look on his face didn't disappear.

"Not bad." Owen brightened. "Garcia used to work for the city before he started his own company. He has a good idea of what grows when, what looks good with each season. The results should be great, once we get that far."

Sitting back, he said. "Enough hotel stuff. Tell me more about your new friend, Natália. Maybe you should invite her and her husband to dinner one night. You can wow them with your caldo verde and that pork dish you did Monday night."

"Monday." Carla fingered an edge of the gray lace covering the white tablecloth. She drew in a breath and slowly let it out. "Monday feels so long ago."

Owen reached over and squeezed her hand. "Sorry, babe. I shouldn't be blathering about petty stuff at work when you've had so much to deal with." He eyed her cheek where, Carla knew, the bruise still showed despite the make-up she'd heavily applied.

"I want you to talk about work," she said. "It's a relief to talk about ordinary things. Antiques, auctions, hotel plans." She squeezed his hand back, then checked her wrist-watch. *Eight-forty-five.* Part of her wished they could stay here for hours, holding hands, enjoying the candlelight, letting the romance of Portugal seep back into their sensibilities.

Her thoughts veered toward the restaurant next door and the couple with their baby. "Enjoy your life," her doctor had said.

Reluctantly, she said, "Time to go."

Chapter Nineteen - Going, Going, Gone

The Moreira home was a three-story, baroque building with white plaster walls, ornate stonework, wrought iron balconies, and French windows that sent a shimmer of golden light into the deep blue twilight. Senhor Moreira, son of the deceased owner, had come from Porto to arrange the auction and was at the door in a pin-stripe suit, gravely welcoming people.

His heavy-lidded eyes under a lined forehead and receding hairline conveyed an air of weariness as he took first Carla's hand, then Owen's in his neatly-manicured one. Carla guessed he and his rotund little wife were both in their fifties. In contrast to her husband, Senhora Moreira had bright, inquisitive eyes and a way of cocking her head and moving her shoulders that made Carla think of an elegantly dressed sparrow.

"I wonder what will happen to such a stately old building after this is over," Carla murmured to Owen. They followed Senhora Moreira down a short hall where pale rectangles on the walls remained from paintings that had been removed for the auction. Her left foot throbbed a little, so they walked slowly, their footsteps echoing on the polished wood floor until they came to a small atrium with a glassed-in ceiling framing the twilit sky above.

French doors were opened wide onto the large garden patio filled with rows of folding chairs, most of them occupied by patiently waiting bidders. Rose bushes bordered the wall. At one end a large magnolia tree spread its branches, the scent of its waxy blossoms wafting into the atrium.

Inside, a table was covered with information forms, and a box of bidding paddles sat next to an ornate cash register. Through a side room's doorway, Carla glimpsed assorted furniture, lamps, old trunks, paintings, dishes, boxes of smaller mementos. When she had come earlier to view the Da Silva Porto paintings, the articles were scattered throughout the house to show them off. Now two men were doing a final check of lot tags. The burlier of the two lifted a rosewood and leather library chair as if it were a step-stool and set it beside a library table.

"The paintings are lot number twelve," Carla told Owen. "After that, we can leave."

The cashier, a young woman with a cloud of reddish hair, gave Carla an information card to fill out, and Carla duly recorded her company's credit information. Philomena Resendes, the auctioneer from Porto, stood to one side, checking her gold wristwatch. Her dark hair was in an elegant twist. Her dove-gray pencil skirt and delicate jersey were set off with Luis Onofre shoes, which, Carla noticed admiringly, had a gilt stripe above the heel. With a nod to Carla, Senhora Resendes turned her attention to the garden, no doubt gauging expressions on her bidders' faces and doing mental arithmetic.

The cashier slapped a label with Carla's information on a bidding paddle marked at the top with a large, red, number fifty-seven. Carla felt the familiar excitement auctions always inspired in her. It wasn't the first time she thought bidding must be a little like betting on a favorite in a horse race. Small wonder that, back home, Owen and his friends had a betting pool on which horse might be the next Triple Crown winner.

The patio twinkled with swags of lights along each side, giving almost a festive air to the occasion. As she and Owen threaded their way to two empty seats at one end of the third row, Carla spied across the aisle the man she'd seen exit Costa's shop Monday—the man in the news photo Detective Fernandes had shown her the next day.

Pereira's friend. The vintner. What was his name? *Vitore.*

Vitore was fingering his goatee with one hand, brow furrowed, while he checked the smart phone in his other hand. He looked up and caught Carla's stare. A smile flickered and was gone. Did he recognize her from last week's viewing of auction items? Or had he noticed her after all, Monday, when she stood across from Costa's shop, camera poised, waiting for a clear shot of the azulejo tiles?

She quickly looked away and sat down, unsettled. Fernandes had also said everyone with any connection to the case was a suspect. That meant Vitore was a suspect. He'd been in the shop the day of Costa's murder. He'd looked pretty angry when he left the shop. *How angry?*

"Okay, what is it?" Owen's whisper broke into her thoughts. "I can hear wheels turning."

Staring straight ahead, restraining her desire to peer around at Senhor Vitore, she murmured, "Without being obvious, have a look at the man at the end of the next side row. The one with the Colonel Sanders beard. He's wearing a navy blazer."

"Yeah, I see him; what about him?"

"He's the guy in the photo Fernandes showed us, remember? Pereira's friend. Maybe Costa's enemy."

"Carla . . .." Owen draped an arm over her shoulder and tickled her earlobe. "Leave everything to the police, okay? We're here for the auction."

"I just pointed him out, that's all."

"And you think he's suspicious," Owen said. "Your friend Paulo is the one you should wonder about." He grinned. "On second thought, don't. Don't wonder about anyone."

Senhora Resendes stepped through the door before Carla could reply. Speaking into her handheld microphone in a melodious voice, the auctioneer started the proceedings, first in Portuguese, then in English: "Boa noite, senhoras e senhores, o leilão começará agora. Good evening, ladies and gentlemen, the auction will begin now."

The shorter of the two men Carla had seen arranging lots brought out an elegant eight-day mantelpiece clock—a Waterbury. Carla caught her breath, swept for a moment in a wave of nostalgia, as bidders began vying for the clock.

One of her fondest memories was the Waterbury clock on the mantelpiece in her grandmother's bungalow in Berkeley. Carla had thought it so beautiful, with its gilt feet and the slender marble column on each side of the face. When she was small, Nana would let her wind it with a clunky key. When Carla came to live with her after her parents' automobile accident, Nana let her keep it in her room. It had been a strange consolation, but the clock's sturdiness and beauty, the regularity of its ticking, suggested some order to a world suddenly thrown into chaos. It comforted her. Even now it was on the mantelpiece in Piedmont, waiting for her and Owen's return after the hotel's grand opening in September. A legacy for their own son or daughter when they came of age.

If we have children. For a moment, she let herself wonder how Owen would feel about adoption. The subject hadn't come up in their discussions. In vitro fertilization, yes. From what she had read, that seemed to be the most effective route to go if she couldn't get pregnant.

Still, as Doctor Chan had said, it was too early to consider other options. *Relax; enjoy your life,* Carla reminded herself, then shook away the next thought: *Try to avoid people squeezing your carotid arteries.*

The auctioneer's pronouncement, "Vendido!" brought her back to the present, and she watched the helper carry the clock back into the atrium, followed by the bidder from the audience, a thin woman with frizzy gray hair, clutching her bid paddle like a victory torch.

The next two lots, a nineteenth-century cherry wood sideboard and an 1800 mahogany armoire, each elicited furious bidding. If she weren't here to bid on the paintings for Mrs. Demming, Carla would have been inspired to bid on the sideboard for herself. Owen would go for it. He liked cherry wood as much as she did.

Next was a nineteenth-century, marble-topped game table that was a gem.

Seeing each piece brought out and shown off at its best, was one of Carla's pleasures in attending auctions. That and the additional information she gained about current auction values and budget adjustments for her clients. The scent of roses and magnolias hung in the air. Garden auctions were the most enjoyable.

By the eleventh lot, a pair of Bergmann bronze monkey candlesticks, Carla's curiosity once again drifted to

Vitore. Like her, he hadn't yet bid on anything. She wondered if the deceased Moreira had a wine cellar with rare vintages. Port wines, since this was Portugal. Maybe Vitore was shopping for something to rival his friend Pereira's show-off bottle with the duke's signature. But that would be in a separate, "invitees only" auction, wouldn't it? She hadn't seen any wines or Ports among the lots for tonight.

"Those are weird candlesticks," Owen observed, as a bid of two thousand euros finalized the sale of the bronze monkeys. A wrinkly old man hurried into the atrium, one monkey in each hand, his bid paddle tucked under his arm. "Why didn't you bid on them, babe? Won't they work on Mrs. Demming's mantelpiece?"

"No, no," Carla whispered. "They belong on a table at a party for friends who make monkeys of themselves. One at each end of a gold cloth runner."

"How about at a party for politicians and their monkeyshines?"

Carla giggled. "How about a party for pals that are up to monkey business?"

Senhora Resendes spoke into her microphone again. "Número doze," she said, in her musical voice. "Number twelve."

Carla snapped to attention as the helpers brought out the two Da Silva Porto paintings. Murmurs of appreciation ran around the audience. Senhora Resendes reminded bidders first in Portuguese, then in English, that the deceased owner had wished the paintings to be sold as a pair and that his son was respecting his wish.

She started the bid at forty-thousand euros.

To Carla's surprise, Senhor Vitore lifted his paddle, his expression confident, as if he already owned them.

169

"Quarenta mil euros," Senhora Resendes said. "Tenho quarenta e cinco mil? Do I have forty-five thousand?"

Carla waited to see if anyone else was going to bid. Apparently, someone behind her did.

When the price went up again to fifty thousand, she raised her paddle, and immediately felt Vitore's intent gaze slide toward her, even though his posture didn't change. When Senhora asked for fifty-five thousand, Vitore's paddle went up. Carla bid sixty. He went to sixty-five.

Now they were the only bidders. Carla suddenly wondered just how rich Vitore was. Could he go past a hundred thousand? Mrs. Demming was willing to go to one hundred twenty thousand, but no more.

The bidding climbed to seventy, then seventy-five. She could feel Owen's tense support. He leaned forward, shoulder's hunched, as if silently cheering a favorite horse at Santa Anita.

Vitore went to eighty.

"Tenho oitenta e cinco mil?"

Eighty-five thousand? Carla raised her paddle.

"Noventa? Ninety?"

Senhora Resendes looked in Vitore's direction, waiting.

It seemed to Carla that the air grew very still, as if all the other bidders were waiting, too. She let herself sneak a look at Vitore, her fingers tense on her paddle. What she saw jolted her.

Senhor Vitore took a small foil-wrapped candy from his pocket and began unwrapping it. Even from where she sat, Carla could see the gold glitter of the paper—the kind of paper that was in her handbag, wrapped in Natália's lace-edged handkerchief. He took out the toffee, popped it nervously in his mouth, crumpled the wrapper, then tossed it on the grass at his feet.

It was Vitore! Not Senhora Gonzaga! Carla crossed her legs, jiggling her foot. If only she could get her hands on that wrapper. With both wrappers, she'd have something worth showing to Fernandes.

Vitore lifted his paddle to bid ninety thousand, and Carla heard the intake of several breaths.

"Noventa e cinco mil?" Senhora Resendes cocked her head at Carla.

If ninety thousand made Vitore nervous enough to start popping toffees, he was getting close to his limit. Carla raised her paddle.

"Cem mil euros? One hundred thousand euros?"

Vitore held the auctioneer's eyes a moment, then gave a slight shake of his head.

"Noventa e cinco mil, vendido. Lot twelve sold to number fifty-seven." Philomena Resendes smiled at Carla. Vitore turned to give her a baleful stare.

Hoping her face was expressionless, Carla followed Owen to the aisle as the helpers took the paintings back to the cashier. She kept her eyes on her husband's suit jacket, not letting herself look at the wrapper, not wanting Vitore to know she had noticed it.

Inside, she arranged for shipping, shivering slightly as she remembered the expression on Vitore's face. *Not a man to be crossed, kiddo. Not good.*

In silence, she and Owen walked through the Arco da Porta Nova, back to Rua do Souto and, beyond, the Praça República. They stopped at Café Vianna for a glass of wine. In the vast fountain that dominated the square, streamers of water shot up and splashed down, colored by changing lights, one of Carla's favorite sights. Their table was close enough for her to feel a faint mist.

She looked around, momentarily enjoying the soft hubbub of conversations and clinking glasses, waiters and waitresses rushing back and forth with new orders. The moon had risen higher, now a paler lemon wafer in the wine dark sky. She crossed her ankles and leaned back, trying to relax, as Owen ordered wine.

Her thoughts ricocheted back to Vitore and the realization he was the one leaving wrappers everywhere: the wrapper in Costa's office; the one in her purse. True, Costa could have left the wrapper in his office. But someone else had left the wrapper in the corridor between shops. And now Vitore had tossed a third wrapper on the lawn in Moreira's garden.

There was no getting around it. She would have to call Detective Fernandes. *Tomorrow morning. After Owen leaves for the hotel.*

Owen lit a cigarette. "You're pretty quiet."

"I'm just a little tired," Carla said. How could she tell him what she suspected about Vitore? Hadn't he reminded her all evening—all week, in fact—to leave everything to the police? She reached over and smoothed Owen's lapel.

He put his arm around her waist and planted a light kiss on the cheek that wasn't bruised and she got a whiff of what she liked to think of as his personal blend: Brut and eau de nicotine.

"You're grinning," he said. "What's going on in there?"

"Too complicated to explain."

The waitress brought their wine.

Carla took a sip and closed her eyes, as if that could hold the moment, the gentle mist from the fountain, the murmur of voices, Owen's hand curled around hers.

She gave a mental shrug. She might as well enjoy the present peacefulness before a new scolding from Detective Fernandes.

Chapter Twenty – A Jarring Conversation

"Let me understand this," Fernandes said on the phone. His voice was chilly enough to cause frostbite. Dreading this conversation, Carla had dawdled the morning away, doing a wash, checking her calendar, checking Facebook and email, outlining her article about Torres's shop, and finally organizing the tableware in the kitchen drawer.

She braced herself for a tirade and a new reminder that she should leave detecting to the police.

Instead, Fernandes calmly reiterated the points she had shared. "You went to the side door in the patio space between Senhor Costa's wineshop and the gift shop next door, yes?"

"Yes."

"You found a candy wrapper, yes?"

"Yes."

"You removed it, and it is in your purse, yes?"

"Yes." She decided not to mention Natália found it. No need to get her new friend in trouble.

"And you think it links Senhor Vitore to the death of Senhor Costa, yes?"

"That's why I'm calling you, yes," Carla said, hearing an edge in her voice. "I thought you should know. Senhor Vitore eats these candies when he's nervous."

The detective was silent.

174

"It seemed important to let you know," she repeated, thinking that last comment of hers hadn't quite conveyed what concerned her about Vitore.

"What is important, senhora, is that you removed evidence from the scene of a crime."

"The crime scene tapes in front were gone. How can you say—"

"Every part of the premises is part of the crime scene until this case is solved."

"Oh," Carla said. Why didn't they mention that on TV crime shows or in mystery novels?

She closed her eyes, thinking of the wrapper she'd found in Costa's office and then tossed in his wastebasket. For a terrible moment, she wondered if they had found it with her fingerprints all over it. Well, they hadn't taken her fingerprints when she filled out her statement.

So that's no problem. Or was it? Her fingerprints would be all over the pens he used when she filled out her statement. And they were all over the wineglass she'd set next to the case in Costa's shop.

"I'm just telling you what I observed," she said, deciding to take the offensive. "You should be glad I called. I could have just kept it to myself and avoided this . . . this unpleasantness!" She hoped her voice was as full of reprimand as his had been.

"That would not have been possible. You were seen with your friend going into the corner shop. It is good that you called. If not, I would have called you to ask why you found such a visit necessary."

"I was seen?" Carla was embarrassed by the squeak in her voice.

"And now I wish to know, who is this woman who was with you, and why is she involved?"

"She's a friend," Carla said hotly. "Just a nice, friendly neighbor I unloaded my troubles to, because this has been one hell of a week. And she . . . became interested."

"Interested in this corridor between shops?"

Carla didn't reply.

"What was *your* interest, senhora? What were you doing there?"

"Stop treating me like a criminal," Carla said angrily. "I haven't done anything wrong."

"But you have," Fernandes said calmly. "As I have pointed out. You removed evidence from a crime scene. Evidence we would have found. And at present everyone is a suspect."

"I don't see how you can even *think* I'm a suspect."

"You found the body. You were the last to see Senhor Costa alive. You had an important bottle he was trying to sell back to Pereira. You say O Lobo stole it from you. O Lobo denies it."

"But yesterday you said he said . . ." Carla shook her head to clear her thoughts. "You said he admitted that he was involved and that *he* said Paulo was his partner."

"True, I said that."

Carla frowned. What did Fernandes mean by that?

"Besides," she told him, "Maria saw him steal it!"

"True, Senhorita Santos gave you an alibi, but her namorado, her sweetheart was involved. She gave him the alibi, too, at first."

"Until I persuaded her to come and tell you," Carla said.

"Which can be seen as a smart move on your part."

Carla exploded. "So *that's* why I had a shadow! It wasn't for protection at all! You *lied* to us! You reassured my husband and me, and all the time I was being followed as a suspect. And still am, from what you say!"

"Acalme-se, Senhora Bass. Calm down. I have not said you are being followed. I have only said you were seen. And I am simply pointing out to you that any action can be regarded in many ways until we capture the criminal."

When Carla didn't answer, he said, "You will bring this candy wrapper to the station in half an hour, please. I hope you have not touched it."

In spite of herself, Carla asked, "So if there are fingerprints on the wrapper, can you match them to the killer?"

After a loud sigh that meant, Carla was sure, to convey Fernandes was a patient man, the detective said, "We can match fingerprints on the wrapper *if* the same fingerprints are already in the system. If not . . .." She could almost hear his shrug. "But we must try, yes?"

Since that sounded somewhat conciliatory, she said, "Of course."

"Half an hour," he said, and hung up.

Chapter Twenty-One – Candy Wrappers and Doldrums

At the station, Carla followed the sidewalk down to the lower level and stopped by the enclosed kiosk where the policeman on duty screened visitors. He spoke little English, but flagged down Agent Rios, a young, clean-shaven man with a wiry build. Rios listened gravely as she explained that Detective Fernandes had asked her to bring in a piece of evidence for a case he was handling.

"Come this way." He led Carla past the parked cars, motorcycles, orange trees, and weeping willows to the small building where she'd gone Monday to write out her statement.

Estela was at her desk, on the phone as before, her dark hair bunched in curls on top of her head. Her friendly glance suggested she remembered Carla, but there was no sign of Fernandes. Agent Rios handed Carla a paper and pen and said, "Please write your name, and what you are giving us. The receptionist will give this with your evidence to the detective."

The receptionist. The detective. Between Rios's formality and Fernandes's absence (despite his chilly command to bring the candy wrapper) the message was clear: *Persona non-grata.* She signed the paper and gave the wrapper, still folded in Natália's handkerchief, to Estela, while Rios looked on, arms crossed, a bemused look on his face.

Estela put them in a small plastic bag and labeled it. "Obrigada," she told Carla.

Carla made her steps firm and confident as she left the building, swallowing her disappointment that Fernandes hadn't been in the office. She had hoped that in person she could explain her intentions calmly and reasonably. But now, as she crossed the patio, she could feel the threads of her argument slipping away. What did Fernandes care that she thought Paulo was innocent of murder? To Fernandes, she was just an interfering snoop who read too many mysteries.

The hovering scent of orange blossoms lifted her spirits. Hunger fluttered in her stomach. It wouldn't hurt to stop by Centésima Página for a bite and then see if her book had come in.

When she reached Avenida Central, violin music, dreamy and sad, floated from a doorway. The young woman Carla often saw on various streets, wore a long black dress and a white jacket. She stood playing, eyes closed, the violin case at her feet open for contributions. Carla went over and dropped in a euro before entering the elegant baroque building that housed Centésima Página's bookstore and café.

Helena Veloso, one of the owners, nodded from the register where a customer waited.

Carla spotted the clerk who had placed her order for Cara Black's *Murder in Pigalle*. "Your book is not here," he said. "But it should not be long."

Carla sighed. That could mean tomorrow or next week.

She strolled around the shop for a few minutes. She liked bookstores. The various sections labeled by genre suggested worlds of possibilities, with everything still in place. Centésima Página—Hundredth Page—had books in several languages, and Carla was reminded of last night's conversation about Gabriela's vision for the new hotel's library lounge.

At the cafeteria bar near the door to the garden, she ordered a plate of cheese and a glass of vinho verde. She took her light lunch past small tables lining the hallway to sit at the table where she and Owen had sat Monday.

Taking a small bite of cheese, Carla pondered the fact that someone had spied on her yesterday and reported her to Fernandes. If only she could talk to Bethany. But Bethany was in the San Francisco office—or would be in a few hours. They wouldn't Skype until this evening. Natália worked on Fridays, she remembered. Maria was at Costa's funeral with the newly widowed aunt she disliked. *I wonder how that's going.* But Carla didn't feel up to a conversation with Maria, anyway. It could only lead to Paulo and the many issues surrounding him. For the first time since coming to Braga, Carla was assailed with a sense of loneliness.

Doldrums, she told herself, then perked up. One cure for doldrums never failed. She eyed her newest shoes. True, she'd bought them only two days ago. But it wouldn't hurt to pay another visit to RCC Lux and see if the strawberry pink stilettos were still there.

Chapter Twenty-Two - Shoes, Beautiful Shoes

At RCC Lux, Carla found the sales clerk tapping a finger against her chin, head cocked, as she studied a display of platform wedges with small bunches of plastic berries on each instep. Open-toed stiletto-heeled sandals in various colors surrounded the wedges.

"Boa tarde," she said when she saw Carla. "You are back again!"

"I couldn't stay away," Carla said, noticing the clerk's name tag this time: *Silvia.* She filed that away.

With a chuckle, tossing back her shoulder-length, tawny hair, Silvia said, "Many of our customers have such a problem."

Carla eyed the platform wedges—not her favorite style—and an orange, strappy stiletto sandal next to it. Near the window, a pair of white stiletto sandals with gold straps caught her eye, but they suggested evening wear. The strawberry pink stilettos were gone. She should have bought them as soon as she knew she liked them.

"Do you have anything else?"

"We have been rearranging. I was getting ready to bring more out," Silvia said. She disappeared into the back room and returned with a stack of boxes.

Carla slipped off her shoes. Seeing the folded pad in her left shoe, the clerk looked at Carla in concern.

"You have had an accident?"

"Long story," Carla said, not wanting to go into it. "I bruised my heel a couple of days ago. It's almost okay."

Silvia pursed her mouth philosophically and took the lid off a shoe box. For the next half hour Carla tried on shoes, imagining and discussing with Silvia various colors and styles and their possible effects with various outfits. She fell in love with a lime green pair that had two straps across the arch and an ankle strap. They were enclosed, though, with pointed toes.

"A perfect color for the season," Silvia said.

Carla knew she was going to buy them, but the pleasure of shopping made her try the others on.

"The yellow and gray is smart, yes?"

"With the right outfit," Carla said diplomatically. It seemed a hard-to-match combination. "You'd have to wear them with a single color to make them work." Still, the strap over the arch was in a beautiful swirl. It was tempting.

"The plum, perhaps?"

"Mmm. Something brighter?"

"So, you will not like the brown and tan."

Carla shook her head and took one of the lime green shoes out of the box again, turning it in her hand, this way and that. "Do you have a belt or a handbag to match these?"

"Yes, this color is very popular right now."

She had just finished paying at the counter and was walking toward the door, when a vaguely familiar, buxom young woman walked in. Carla had to think a moment.

Rosa. The waitress at Senhora Gonzaga's café.

"Boa tarde," Carla said, curious about what brought the young waitress into the shop. Shoes at RCC Lux had to be too expensive for her salary.

Rosa looked puzzled. "Boa tarde. Oh," she said. "You come to the café two days ago."

"You remember me?" Carla asked in surprise. Dozens of tourists had to come into the café this time of year, and many of them must have long, blonde hair.

"Yes. Senhora Gonzaga was so trouble because you ask questions about Senhor Costa across the street." Rosa said. "They are friends, and she is still so grieving he is dead."

"I didn't mean to upset her," Carla said. "I don't like questions either," she confided. "The police asked me a lot of them, too, because I found the . . . I discovered Senhor Costa."

Rosa's brown eyes filled with sympathy. "It is upset to all of us. He was nice man. He sometime comes in for café before he opens his shop. And he would tell me all such nice compliments." She preened a little.

Senhora Gonzaga must have loved that. "Don't you work on Fridays?" Carla asked.

"I work only until three. Every day. After lunch is not so busy, and Senhora Gonzaga don't need me."

She eyed Carla's packages. "So, you buy some shoes here? I always come in here to look at shoes after I go to O Belo. I was hoped to find shoes at O Belo, because Segunda-feira, Senhora Gonzaga told me there is sale."

"Segunda-feira?" Carla frowned, sorting through days of the week in Portuguese. "Oh, Second day. Right. Monday." Even though Sunday was Domingo and not "first day." *Just another little fence to jump in learning Portuguese.*

"I don't have time to see all week because of classes," Rosa continued.

"University classes?" Carla wondered if Rosa knew Maria.

Rosa nodded. "I have them on the afternoon. But on Sexta-feira . . . on Fri—"

"Friday," Carla coached, briefly feeling fluent in languages.

"On Friday I don't have class, so today I go to look, but I don't like anything. Monday, Senhora Gonzaga can find nothing to like for herself also. I think there hasn't been nothing good all week." Rosa gave the gold-strapped sandal near the window a covetous glance.

Carla turned Rosa's words over in her mind. When would Senhora Gonzaga have time to look at shoes Monday? According to what she had told the police, she was in the café in the morning, when she saw Paulo go into the wine shop. After Rosa left at three, the proprietress would have to stay until closing time at seven.

But maybe she went out at lunch time and planned to make her purchase after hours if she saw something she liked, Carla reasoned. Many stores were open until eight. She tried to remember if O Belo was one of them.

"Senhora Gonzaga must have gone during her lunch, while you were there," she mused aloud, trying not to sound prying.

"No. It is too busier then. People like to have snacks. She has gone just before lunch to look. And she hurry back before so many people come in."

"That doesn't seem like much time to check out shoes."

"Well, she goes for maybe half hour. Maybe more," Rosa said crinkling her forehead as she considered it. "I was in charge," she added, preening again. "Because I am so . . . so . . .."

"Capable?" Carla suggested, her mind busy with this new information. Rosa nodded.

Hadn't the proprietress said she was in the café all morning? *Why lie, unless you have something to hide?* Maybe Senhora Gonzaga was the one who visited Costa through the souvenir shop the way Carla had envisioned O Lobo or Senhor Vitore slipping in.

Back to the senhora and her foil-wrapped toffees. Carla rolled her eyes. Maybe all of Braga ate foil-wrapped toffees.

"She didn't see anything she liked at O Belo?" she asked, mentally reviewing the street's layout, trying to imagine how Senhora Costa would get into the souvenir shop without Rosa seeing her. The corner was visible from the café.

Rosa shook her head. "No, but she said there are shoes I will like. But I wait too long."

Carla gave a sympathetic "tsk," her thoughts tracing the only route possible: The proprietress would have to set out for Rua dos Chãos, as if heading for Praça da República, Rua do Souto, and O Belo's shop. At the bank, she could turn left, go along Avenida Central to Rua de São Gonçalves, hook around the corner and go up to the street behind Costa's shop.

She wouldn't go through the souvenir shop. Senhor Torres would recognize her. All the proprietors on the street must know each other. She'd enter from the back street. *She'd have a key to the gate.*

185

But then, after doing Costa in, Senhora Gonzaga would have to return to the café by the same circuitous route. Was half an hour enough time for all that?

And how would she carry away the bottle from the broken case? She'd have a purse, but how big a purse?

Rosa eyed Carla's bags again. "What did you buy?" she asked shyly.

Carla smiled. "Shoes and a handbag." At Rosa's inquisitive stare, she opened the bag with the purse.

"My favorite color has always been green.," Rosa said softly. "This is such a pretty green. Don't you agree?"

"It is," Carla agreed, her mind still on Senhora Gonzaga's hypothetical route. Re-considered, it didn't seem likely. The woman was lying, that much was clear, but she was lying for some other reason. That lie had caused Maria no little confusion about what *she* saw Monday, and it had gotten Paulo in deeper trouble than he would have been for just stealing.

I sure would like to know the reason.

Rosa's voice broke into her thoughts. "This has been great to practice my English with you, senhora. How do you say? Have a great day."

Carla smiled again. "You have a great day, too." Since Rosa was already drifting over to the platform sandals with berries, Carla fluttered a wave at Sylvia and left.

Chapter Twenty-Three - Coffee with a Culprit

She almost careened into Senhor Vitore, who stood to one side of the door, away from the parade of shoppers, his hands clasped behind his back, as if waiting. Carla side-stepped him just in time. Vexed, she said, "Desculpe-me," suspecting she was pronouncing it wrong. She didn't like his smirk, either, as he smoothed the hair neatly fringing his nape. What was he doing here? Not waiting for her, surely.

But he was. With an appraising glance that in the space of a second traveled from her hair to her turquoise and black heels, came back up to rest briefly on her bosom, and then flicked to her face, he asked, "May we talk?"

A shiver ran through her. She thought back to Monday, when she saw him angrily exit Costa's shop. His glance had swept over her then. Maybe he did remember her standing in front of the café with her camera. His last stare at the auction had been one of animosity over her outbidding him for the paintings. Which of those two moments made him want to talk to her?

Before she could say anything, he said, "About the Da Silva Porto paintings. Perhaps we can discuss them over an espresso. Or do you prefer tea?"

Carla was tempted to refuse him outright with a simple "no thank you" and go on her way. Instead she said,

"The Da Silva Porto paintings? I don't know what there is to discuss."

"They have good coffee at A Brasileira," he said, cupping her elbow.

Curiosity overcame her wariness. True, arrows and candy wrappers were pointing to him again, but it was broad daylight and they weren't in some dim hallway. *What can happen with so many people around?* She might learn something.

Shifting the shoulder strap of her handbag as a polite way to disengage her elbow, Carla let herself fall into step beside him, darting cautious glances at him. She was sure this was about more than paintings.

A Brasileira was crowded. It was one of Braga's oldest cafés, situated at the corner of Rua do Souto and Rua de São Marcos. The name meant "The Brazilian Woman." A poster on the corner column of the café under the blue-tiled façade showed a picture of an old woman in a green dress with the words "O melhor café é" over the stylized portrait, and "d'A Brasileira" below it. *The best coffee is from the Brazilian woman.*

They sat outside at a corner table under a white umbrella. Outside tables had a view of the Praça República and Carla found herself idly watching a new crowd of tourists at the distant fountain. Vitore waved a waitress over with an air of authority. From the way they bantered in Portuguese, he must be a frequent customer. He had to be well-known, Carla reminded herself. Detetive Fernandes had said Vitore was from Braga, though he lived in Porto now and only came up to Braga for the occasional auction, or maybe to visit friends.

He wore the same smartly cut navy blazer that he'd worn last night over designer jeans. He was friends with Pereira, she reminded herself. She thought back to the news article Fernandes had shown her and Owen Tuesday evening in the apartment, the one with the picture of Vitore eyeing Pereira's treasured bottle.

As Vitore talked with the waitress, she noticed slight pouches under his eyes that suggested dissipation. His mouth was petulant and wore a disdainful expression when he wasn't smiling. Maybe the waitress found this attractive, mistaking it for confidence. Carla pinched her lips, finding him thoroughly distasteful.

He would know where Pereira kept the duke's bottle in the cellar.

"Espresso," she said when Vitore asked her, and he ordered one for each of them.

"A pastry?" he suggested. "I'm having a pastel de nata."

"No, thank you." The small, flaky egg tarts were quickly becoming one of Carla's favorite sweets, but she didn't want this conversation turning cozy.

The waitress hurried off. Vitore cleared his throat. "About the paintings," he began. "You must have a comfortable budget. I was surprised you could buy the pair."

Impeccable English. "My client is the one with the comfortable budget," Carla said. "I'm an interior designer. The paintings are for her home in Belvedere. California," she added. "In the United States."

"I know where California is." He favored her with a disarming grin. "Now. The paintings. If it were not for the stone lions I wanted for my garden in Porto, I would have bought the paintings to go with one I already have. But

189

perhaps you will sell one of them to me. Then I will have at least a pair."

So. This is *about the paintings.*

His dark brown eyes gleamed with hidden depths, unfathomable. *Secretive eyes. Sly.* He reminded her of a fox. He seemed to be waiting, but for what?

She was glad the waitress brought their order at that moment so that she could compose her thoughts while he counted out the change on the tray—no tip, she noticed. *Cheapskate.* She made a mental note to wait until he left and then leave a tip of her own. He tore open two of the square packets of sugar showing miniature portraits of the Brazilian woman, then poured the sugar in his cup, stirring it briskly and setting the small spoon to one side.

After a sip from her own cup, enjoying the bitter tang she always savored, Carla said, "I can't sell you one of the paintings. They were sold as a pair because the previous owner wanted them to remain that way."

Vitore made a dismissive gesture with a thrust of his goatee and took a bite of his pastel de *nata.*

"And my client fell in love with them as a pair, when I sent pictures to her. It's part of the look we've envisioned for her entry hall."

Another dismissive jab of the goatee.

"But even if I wanted to sell one, which I don't," Carla said, resenting his attitude that any impediment to his wish list was negligible, "they've been picked up for shipping." They wouldn't be until tomorrow, but he didn't need to know that.

"Ah well." Vitore shrugged. "Assim é a vida, yes? Such is life. So, we must talk of other things. How are you enjoying Portugal?" He sipped his espresso and regarded her with his fox's eyes. "How long will you be here? Has anyone shown you around our beautiful city? Do you need a guide?"

Is he hitting on me? Carla lifted her cup with her left hand so that her wedding band showed. "I'm in good hands for seeing Braga," she said. "My neighbor has taken me under her wing. But to answer your first question, I love Braga. It's full of charm."

"Full of charm, yes. But," Vitore wrinkled his brow as if a thought had just occurred to him. "I am guessing you have had an un-charming experience. I think you are the one who found the owner of Adega do Costa dead in his shop. It was in the newspaper Tuesday morning."

Carla felt the hairs on her neck go on stand-up alert. She made her eyes wide—artless, she hoped—and asked, "What newspaper was that?"

"*O Examinador.*"

Tuesday, in the Jardim de Santa Bárbara, the article Maria had translated only mentioned Costa was found dead by a customer and that a three-thousand-euro bottle had been stolen from a smashed case. Why would Vitore decide she was the customer who found Costa?

"I don't know Portuguese," Carla said. "What else did the newspaper say?"

"That an American woman was returning an expensive bottle to him, but when she went into the shop she found him dead."

"Yes, that was me," Carla said, controlling her unease. The newspaper hadn't said anything about an American woman returning a bottle.

"And a thief stole the bottle she was returning."

Bingo! I was right. This isn't about the paintings.

191

Not trusting her voice, Carla looked down, then shook her head and sighed as if plagued by the memory. She was sure now that she was sitting across from O Lobo's employer. The one who had arranged the whole bottle-switch thing. *And maybe more.*

"I'm curious," Vitore said. "Why were you returning the bottle?"

"It wasn't the Port I bought. I bought a tawny Port. This was something different. I think he put it in my bag by mistake."

"Ah." Vitore finished his pastel de nata and dabbed the corners of his mouth with the small paper napkin, then wiped his fingers and brushed at his mustache as if it might hold crumbs.

A careful man. When he's not dropping candy wrappers.

"You must have had a good look at it when you took it out of the bag." Again, the sly eyes watching her, waiting. "What did it look like?"

Carla lifted her shoulders. "Really old, from the label. And someone had scribbled all over it. It wasn't the one I'd bought, for sure, so I brought it back."

"The newspaper said it was expensive," he pursued.

"If it was expensive, it wouldn't be in my budget," Carla quipped, relieved to feel her mettle returning.

"Perhaps your wealthy client's budget?"

A disbelieving laugh escaped Carla. Did he think she was returning to Costa's shop to make some kind of a deal with him? *Oh, please.* Although, given what she'd learned about Costa, the wine-seller probably would be open to deals. Vitore would know that. To people like Vitore, probably everyone was open to double-crossing someone else.

"My client is a teetotaler," she told him.

"Teetotaler?"

"She doesn't drink. She wouldn't be into expensive Port, if that's what it was."

Vitore said mildly, "Even a wealthy teetotaler might like to show off an expensive Port." He glanced at his espresso and took a sip.

At his wording, Carla had to look away. Senhor Costa's flirty voice revived in her head, saying, in his quirky English, "People like to show off."

Recovering her composure, Carla said, "My client wouldn't want to show off a bottle or anything else. She likes beautiful things for her house, that's all."

There was something not right about the turn of conversation. Maybe Vitore *didn't* think deal-making was in the picture. He was trying to find out something else. But what?

"An expensive Port like the newspaper mentioned," he remarked. "It seems a strange mistake. I wonder what happened to it."

Bingo again. Three puzzle pieces fell into place for Carla: Vitore didn't know O Lobo was in jail. Sure, a man had been arrested for attacking a woman in a café, but the police wouldn't have publicized who the attacker was. Fernandes wouldn't, anyway. Not yet. That wasn't how he did things.

O Lobo was holding the stolen bottle for Vitore. And now Vitore's looking for it, wondering why it isn't in O Lobo's apartment. The next thought came to her as clearly as if in neon lights: Vitore was the anonymous party Fernandes had mentioned Wednesday—the one who had found out his own bottle was a fake.

"I didn't realize it was an expensive bottle," Carla said, giving her eyelashes a little flutter. "This whole thing has been so upsetting." Feeling she had nothing to lose by her next comment, she added, "Senhor Costa got a phone call when I was in the shop."

"A phone call?" A tightness had come into Vitore's voice. She'd bet anything he'd made the call.

"While I was looking around at his wines," Carla said. "He had a nice selection," she added, making her tone chatty. "I was tempted to buy the ruby Port as well as the tawny, but—"

Vitore leaned forward, "But he never mentioned this particular bottle to you? The one you were returning? Told you where he got it?"

"Why would he? I was just shopping for a nice Port. I wanted the one I bought from him, not this other bottle."

Vitore sat back and drummed the table with manicured nails. "And he put it in your bag, and you knew nothing about it," he mused. "And you weren't curious?"

"Not until I got home," Carla said. She eyed his spoon lying to one side and gave herself a mental pat on the back for not giving anything away—that she knew the thief was O Lobo, that she knew forgeries were floating around, and that in a few moments she would have new evidence linking Vitore to everything that had happened.

"I took the bottle back right away," she said, still in the flow of her tale, "but it was too late. When I got to the shop, he was dead."

Vitore reached over and patted her hand, switching suddenly to her solicitous friend, an earnest look on his face. "Not too late. Think. If you had arrived when the killer was there." He let his puckered brows convey the rest.

Carla nodded solemnly, as if she believed his concern was real. Then she took a sip from her cup and swallowed, closing her eyes to convey she was having an espresso moment, hoping he'd take the hint and leave. She opened them again. In a sugary voice, she said, "They're certainly right when they boast they have the best coffee." She purposely kept her gaze on her cup, where a tiny portrait in the ceramic surface matched the one on the torn sugar packet.

"Yes. The coffee is very good." Vitore drained his cup, dabbed his mouth again, and stood. "I have taken too much of your time. It is a pity we could not come to an arrangement about the paintings, but I have enjoyed the pleasure of your company." He winked. "Perhaps we will see each other again at another auction."

"Perhaps." Carla flashed him a smile. *Not if I can help it, buddy!* "Thank you for the espresso," she said.

As soon as he turned and started strolling back up Rua do Souto toward the Arco da Porta Nova, she wrapped her paper napkin around the small spoon he had handled and scooped it into her purse. She took out her notebook with its pen on a string, snapped the purse shut, and hung the strap on the back of her chair again. She massaged her forehead, running the strange conversation through her mind. She needed to write this down, put it in order.

Vitore was involved, for sure. *Vittore's interested in the bottle O Lobo took,* she scribbled. *He made up lies about what the newspaper said.* She wrote that down. He had to be O Lobo's mysterious employer, the one O Lobo only called from public phones to keep their conversations untraceable. She didn't write down that last, but she smiled to herself. Vitore wouldn't be untraceable after she stopped by the police station with the spoon he had handled. If prints on it matched the prints on the wrapper—and Carla was sure they would—Fernandes would have new questions for O Lobo to answer.

O Lobo will have to tell the truth this time. She steepled her fingers, then couldn't resist letting her toes do a little happy dance under the table. Brushing her hair back with one hand, she took a last sip of espresso and turned to retrieve her handbag and leave a tip for the waitress.

Her handbag was gone.

Chapter Twenty-Four – Realizations

For a moment, Carla was too stunned to move. Everything was in her handbag—passport, wallet, credit cards, cash, phone, camera. She looked around wildly, hoping to spot the thief, but the street was busy with tourists walking at cross purposes, some headed for shopping further up Rua do Souto, others walking toward the Praça da República, consulting guidebooks.

A white standard poodle, elegantly groomed, strained at its leash, tugging a breathless brunette in a yellow shift toward the Arco da Porta Nova. Two teen-age boys bantered with a group of giggling girls. A gray-haired couple strolled hand in hand, the man adjusting his straw trilby, the woman in a flowered dress and low-heeled bone pumps. Two other women walked by, arm in arm, their similar faces generational, a mother and daughter. The young woman who had earlier played her violin on Avenida Central was a few doors away, bending to take her instrument out of its case.

No one looked like a thief. *But what does a thief look like?* They wouldn't all look like O Lobo.

Someone who knew what they were doing. For a paranoid moment, Carla wondered if Vitore had loitered in a doorway and seen her snatch his spoon. If so, he'd know she suspected him. A chilling thought. But, no, she had watched him walk toward the Arco da Porta Nova, his back to her.

A pickpocket, then. Of all times, why did a pickpocket have to settle on her? Today? At that moment? She should

197

never have hung her purse on the back of her chair. She felt like slapping her head, but then she'd look even more like the idiot she felt.

Instead of cleverly turning in a genuine piece of evidence against Vitore, now she had to report a stolen purse. After that, she'd have to stop by the hotel and get Owen's key to the apartment. She'd have to go around scaffolding and drop cloths, hoping he wasn't in the middle of a meeting when she did find him. And then they would have to start making phone calls to change credit cards, not to mention contacting the U. S. embassy to report and replace her passport.

Damn, damn, damn!

Wearily she trudged back to Campo de São Tiago, clutching her little notebook in one hand, the package with her new shoes and purse bumping against her leg, suddenly much too bulky. For once, as she retraced her steps along the slanting sidewalk down to the kiosk in the car-filled plaza, Carla wished she didn't wear stilettos.

The same officer was in the kiosk.

"I want to report a stolen purse," Carla told him. No matter that he didn't speak English. Recognizing her from this morning, he made a quick phone call, and a moment later Agent Rios came walking briskly from one of the far offices.

"Yes, this way, please," he told her. This time he had decided she deserved a cordial smile. He led her back to the sterile office where she'd returned the candy wrapper this morning. To her surprise, Fernandes was leaning against an office door, chatting with Estela.

"Ah! Senhora Bass," he said. "How convenient that you have come. I have something I believe you want." He went through a door in the back and returned a moment later with her handbag. "Someone found this a few minutes ago and turned it in. I hope you will forgive us for opening it to ascertain who owned it."

"I was coming to report it," Carla said slowly, trying to wrap her head around this new development. "Someone stole it. Not more than twenty minutes ago."

"You are in luck, then. Please take a seat and fill out a report, and we will be happy to return it." He pulled a chair close to Estela's desk. "Make sure all your belongings are in it and nothing was taken," he added. Behind his usual sober expression, Carla could almost swear there was a gleam in his eye.

She sat, awareness of Detetive Fernandes's steady gaze prickling her neck as she filled out the paper Estela handed her. Before signing, Carla riffled through her purse to check that everything was there. The spoon was gone. *Of course. Just another way to say, "Butt out of this case."* No way was he going to give her the satisfaction of turning in a legitimate clue.

"Anything missing?" Fernandes asked. She looked up. In the glance they shared, it was clear that he knew.

"No," she snapped. "Everything's in order." She signed the paper and handed it to him, then slung the strap over her shoulder.

With a polite nod, he said, "Have a good afternoon."

On the way home, walking along Avenida Central, Carla fumed with every step. Fernandes had said she wasn't being followed, but, obviously, she was. Her new shadow had seen her take the spoon—evidence—and immediately took it to Fernandes. *The tail who's been following me, not for protection, but because I'm a suspect.*

Unless . . .. Her steps slowed.

199

Unless Vitore was the one being followed. Carla stood stock still.

Fernandes must have suspected Vitore even before she called this morning. But he wouldn't let her know that. *He isn't going to let anyone know anything.* Now she wished she hadn't been so quick to leave the station. Maybe she should have told him about Vitore's questions. Whoever took her purse and the spoon wasn't privy to their conversation unless they had incredibly good ears. Should she call Fernandes?

Uh-uh. The candy wrapper had only earned her a scolding. Now that Fernandes had the spoon, it was up to him. If he wanted to know what Vitore said to her, he could ask Vitore. She was through volunteering anything.

At least they can match prints on the spoon against those on the wrapper. Maybe Vitore wasn't in the system, but if the ones on the spoon matched the ones on the wrapper, it would prove he had been lurking around Costa's shop for some reason. The case might be solved. She could get back to her life.

Church bells tolled the half-hour. Carla checked her watch— five-thirty. Her Skype conference with Bethany was in thirty minutes.

"The Duartes want more information on the price of azulejo tiles," Bethany told her as soon as Carla updated her about shipments of the paintings and mirror. "Can you come up with a price list?"

"It's not that simple. I'd have to know what patterns they have in mind. These are hand-painted. They come in different styles and colors; mostly blue and white and yellow, but other colors, too. Some are geometrical, some meant to create scenes. Some of them take months to paint, fire, and deliver." Carla said. "Have they mentioned a budget? Do they have a color scheme?"

"They like the blue and white ones you've shown in posts," Bethany said.

"Okay. Traditional."

"I asked them about tiling the baths. They like that. Also, now they're talking about having a fountain in the back patio and tiling it in azulejos. But they also want something economical."

"Economical these aren't. I can send catalogues from various companies, but the Duartes may be a lost cause if that's a serious issue."

"Okay. But we have another new client."

"A desirable one, from the look on your face."

"Another wealthy widow. Mrs. Weatherby in Atherton. She has Portuguese and French ancestry, but her husband's heritage was English." Bethany twirled a lock of short hair. "She lives in a mansion. I took a side trip to meet her in Atherton on the way to Carmel."

"Ah. Carmel. How's our orthodontist coming along?"

"I think he's satisfied with the suggestions I made. The walk-through went well, and he likes the material and wallpaper samples I took." Bethany glanced away, a private smile playing about her mouth. "There's some wall changes that have to be made," she said, looking at Carla again. "I've contacted an architect in the area."

"Sounds good. So, tell me more about our Mrs. Weatherby. What's her house like? And what's she looking for?"

"They went for the English Country look when her husband was alive. A lot of Chintz. White ceilings all through. Intricate moldings She wants to keep those. The rest is pretty traditional. But now she wants to go with her own heritage in a remodel. She was clicking around the Internet, and our website came up with your photos of the azulejo tiles in the Old Archbishop's Palace that you wrote about last month. She can afford them, too, from what I've seen. Looks like we could end up with lots of Portuguese-heritage clients in the future, the way things are going."

"Hmm. French and Portuguese. And she likes the white ceilings. We could go French country, since she likes flowered furniture. Even French classic. Tiles could work with either one if she's keeping the white ceilings. We could tile the entry hall and baths. And frame any fireplaces," Carla said. "Those are perfect places to show azulejo tiles off. How many bathrooms?"

"Four."

"That might be overkill, unless we just use the tiles as accent pieces in one or two of the baths."

"She wants to meet you. Should I ask Jessica to set up an appointment with her and then book a flight for you in a couple of weeks?"

"I wish!" Carla felt the familiar excitement of a new project. This one was appealing for its blend of cultures combined in old world elegance. *Not to mention getting miles away from dead bodies, shady vintners, snooty detectives . . ..* "I can't, though." Hadn't Fernandes told her not to leave Portugal until the case was solved?

Carla jutted her chin, a flare of rebellion stirring inside. But she'd have to abide by the order. Owen had the hotel project to finish. That was why they were here in the first place. She couldn't do anything to put him in a bad light with this employer.

"Can you handle it?" she asked Bethany. "I can send you the catalogues for starters."

"Honey, you know I can, but it's your post that caught her attention. This should be your baby. You should have seen your face light up at the prospect."

"This stupid case isn't solved yet."

"Don't tell me!" Bethany sat back. "You're still—"

"A suspect, yeah," Carla made a face, remembering how clearly Fernandes had spelled that out for her. "I think they're close to solving the case. Just not close enough for me to make any plans."

"Jeez." Bethany's face grew grave.

"They caught someone involved, and they're watching people, but they're still searching for the killer. I may even have had coffee with him today," Carla couldn't help adding.

Bethany's swallowed several times as Carla told her about seeing Vitore while she photographed the shop Monday, then his behavior at the auction, and again today when they had coffee.

"Have you told the police?"

"They know," Carla said sourly. She told Bethany about the candy wrapper and the spoon.

"You went into this shop next door and pretended to be writing an article?" Bethany snorted, then shook her head. "Portugal is having quite an effect on you. What's this article supposed to be about?"

"Old buildings. I'm really going to write it on my blog."

"Oh. Yeah. I can see that. Good idea."

"My neighbor's idea. But it worked. We found the wrapper I told you about."

"Detective what's-his-name should be shaking your hand," Bethany said.

"He isn't."

"I read recently where they caught a teen-age robber because of a candy-wrapper."

"That's good news," Carla said, "although his prints probably were already in the system."

"Ooh, you sound so private investigator-ish." Bethany cocked her head. "That must come from hanging out with your detective friend."

"I don't hang out with him, and he's not my friend. He hates me," Carla said.

"So, has your candy wrapper man been arrested?"

"Not yet."

"Does he think you suspect him?"

"I hope not."

"Be careful, honey. He doesn't sound like someone to take lightly."

"He's not the only one," Carla said. She told Bethany about O Lobo's attack on her. Her friend's look of horror made her wish she had left that incident out.

"Carla, what have you gotten yourself into?"

"He's locked up," Carla assured her. "He won't be running off with stolen bottles anytime soon."

"Stamping on his foot!" Bethany smiled wryly. "I'll have to remember that if someone tries to mug me in a parking lot." Still, she looked worried.

"You don't wear stilettos, so it might not work," Carla said, then narrowed her eyes.

"What?"

"Just a thought that came to me. About shoes. It's probably irrelevant." Having coffee with Vitore and fielding his questions had made her forget her conversation with Rosa.

"What is it you're not telling me?"

"Nothing."

"What kind of nothing?" Bethany leaned forward.

Carla rolled her eyes. "You worry too much. Instead, why don't you find out if Mrs. Weatherby is on Skype. If so, send me an e-mail address, and then we can meet online."

"Okay, but honey, this isn't one of your mystery novels. It's real life. Stay out of it."

Bethany's warning hung in the air after they hung up.

Carla's fingernails made a rat-a-tat-tat against the desk's chestnut finish. She really should stay out of it. The police had O Lobo. Now they had evidence that Vitore was involved. Paulo was the chump in this picture. She was sure Vitore had planned the bottle switch. His thug, O Lobo, had found Paulo to carry out the switch. Vitore or O Lobo had killed Costa. A few moments ago, she might have put her money on Vitore, but actually O Lobo seemed more likely. She could imagine Vitore making threats—the phone call to Costa, for instance. Vitore could have sent O Lobo to scare Costa into telling where the duke's bottle was. Maybe even telling him to rough Costa up if necessary. *And O Lobo lost control, because he's probably that kind of guy.* Vitore might have come back later to see if O Lobo had left anything that could incriminate him. *And left the candy wrapper.*

Carla chewed her lip. The more she thought about things, the less sure she was that arresting Vitore would help Paulo. Instead, Vitore might help O Lobo pin Costa's death on Paulo. Sure, the police could get Vitore for swindling Pereira. But that was a lesser crime with a lesser penalty.

Senhora Gonzaga's the only one who could help Paulo.

And she lied about him. Why? Even if Costa was worried about Paulo romancing his niece, and Senhora Gonzaga had felt Paulo was a playboy, it was none of that woman's business. Thanks to her, Paulo was a murder suspect.

Carla pinched her chin between her thumb and forefinger. Should she call Fernandes and tell him Senhora Gonzaga lied?

And get chewed out again?

It would be better to get Senhora Gonzaga to tell him she lied. But how?

The front hall door closed. A moment later Owen came into the room. He walked over, kissed her on the lips, lifted her off the chair, and twirled her around, a Cheshire Cat grin making his dimples even more pronounced.

"Good day, huh?" she asked, catching her breath as he set her down.

"We have a new applicant for the night clerk position," he said. "He speaks Portuguese and three other languages. Gabriela likes the idea of expanding the book collection. And Tiago is talking to a potential chef."

Carla smiled. "What's not to like?"

Owen hooked his thumbs his pockets, something that Carla always found sexy because of the way it made his pants hang on his hips. "And how was your day?" he asked.

Carla mentally riffled through the day's events. "Business is picking up at home. We have a new client. And," she smiled up at him. "I bought new shoes."

"Why am I not surprised?"

"And I had coffee with my competitor from last night," she slipped in.

"The vintner?" Owen looked startled. "What was his name again?"

"Vitore."

Owen gave a soft whistle. "How did that come about?"

"He was waiting for me when I came out of RCC Lux."

"He followed you?" Owen's cheer vanished.

"I think it was just coincidence," she said, not wanting to worry him. "I think he spotted me through the window and saw a chance to talk to me. He wanted me to sell him one of the paintings."

"What's he like up close and personal?"

"A jerk. He also was interested in the bottle O Lobo stole from me."

"He brought the theft up with you?" Owen's voice ascended a note. "And you think this is coincidence?" He rubbed his forehead, then ran his hand through his hair. "I don't like the sound of this. He asks you to coffee supposedly to buy a painting, but quizzes you about a bottle everyone seems to be looking for? A bottle Costa was killed for? Or with?"

"He left when I couldn't tell him anything," Carla said.

"First this O Lobo guy grabs you by the neck. Now this vintner is asking questions. I don't think you're taking this seriously enough."

"Okay, okay. Let's not get into an argument—"

"You've told Detective Fernandes, right? He knows Vitore is following you?"

Carla put both hands on her hips. "Of course he knows!" She heard her own voice start up the scale, one word at a time. "Fernandes is all knowing, with eyes everywhere. Meanwhile, I can't even leave the country to go meet the new client Bethany told me about."

"Don't get mad at me because you don't like Fernandes," Owen said. "I'm just worried about your safety. Shouldn't I care what happens to you?"

"You don't have to yell!"

"You don't either!"

They glared at each other.

"I need to start dinner," Carla snapped. She went into the kitchen and took a pot from the cupboard near the sink, banging it down on the counter. As she measured out a cup of rice, she heard him go into the bedroom, closing the door loudly.

And he's not a door slammer, she told herself remorsefully.

The menu she'd planned, tomato rice and shrimp with hot, red peppers, was one of Owen's favorite Portuguese dishes. Thinking of how happy he had looked when he came home, she felt like kicking herself. She'd probably ruined his appetite, wrecked his evening, and all because she was sick of Fernandes and how her life had been turned upside down.

She'd apologize later, at supper. *He needs to cool down first, anyway.*

She covered the rice with two cups of water, adding salt, then took the shrimp from the refrigerator and began peeling them, recriminations swirling in her head. If only she hadn't paused at the corner Monday to photograph those damned tiles. If she hadn't sampled the damned Port. If she hadn't *bought* the damned Port. The whole week could have been so different.

But it wasn't. And now she had to find some way for Fernandes to learn Senhora Gonzaga had lied to him.

If Maria and I went to her together . . . and Senhora Gonzaga realized that Costa's killers could go free . . . . *She would hardly want that to happen.*

Carla pursed her lips. Senhor Costa's funeral had been this afternoon. Tomorrow morning she'd call Maria. Once she explained this latest development, she was sure Maria would want to accompany her to the café.

Chapter Twenty-Five – Can We Talk?

Carla breathed in the fresh morning air, walking along Avenida Central, enjoying the sense of tranquility that washed through her. Last night, after Owen and she had both apologized, they talked late into the night, falling asleep later, holding each other close. At present, Owen was at his office in the hotel, as he was every Saturday morning when the workmen weren't there. When he finished his work, they planned to have lunch at Casa Estaroles, a cozy, family-run restaurant half a street away from their apartment, then drive up to Bom Jesus do Monte—a tourist spot on their must-see list ever since their arrival. According to the brochure, the church, Good Jesus of the Mountain, high in the hills, had fountains, hidden grottoes, gardens, sculptures, and endless vistas. *The perfect peaceful afternoon after a week from hell!* Carla thought.

She shook away a prick of guilt for not telling Owen her morning's plan. She had wavered over dishes about whether to call Detetive Fernandes instead of Maria. But what was the point in talking to Fernandes before she knew why Senhora Gonzaga had lied? Two women could find that out easier than a policeman. Hadn't the detective said that a woman was more likely to confide in a woman? Hadn't she already proved that? The proprietress didn't like Paulo, but she probably didn't realize how much trouble she'd made for him. It was up to Carla to make her understand. She quickened her step, enjoying the sound of her new lime green stilettos clicking on the small, gray and white paving stones.

Maria was waiting by the souvenir shop on the corner, as they had agreed. Her hair was in a French braid this morning, and she fingered it absently, lost in thought. She smiled wanly as Carla approached. The shop was already open. Torres was busy with a customer at his counter, but he nodded at Carla through the open doorway.

"Are you okay?" Carla asked, taking in the dark circles around Maria's eyes and the lines of grief etched at the corners. Funerals and burials had a way of bringing death crushingly home. At her own parents' funeral, Carla had been too numb to pay attention to the minister's words, but when the caskets were lowered into the ground and she had thrown her clumps of dirt, she had felt engulfed in loss. It was only Nana's quiet strength and understanding, her way of respecting Carla's silences and giving her small tasks to perform that had helped Carla manage the first weeks.

Now she wondered if she'd done the wrong thing, asking Maria to accompany her to question Senhora Gonzaga about Paulo. Still, Maria had a right to know why the woman had fingered Paulo, and Carla needed Maria's help to find out. Putting out a tentative feeler, Carla said, "I'm sorry to pull you away from your family at such a sad time."

"I am glad to come away," Maria said. "Everyone is angry or sad. My mother keeps crying. My uncle was her older brother. He always look . . . looked out for her. Now there is only her. My aunt says ugly things about my uncle. She is afraid he has left money to his other woman, because there is a will. My father says not to yell at my mother. But he shouts this. It is all terrible."

"Isn't there always a will?"

211

Maria shook her head. "Normally my aunt would share everything in equal parts with her two sons. But a lawyer has asked the family to meet with him Monday. Someone else is going to get something." Maria's lip curled. "That is her only concern. She does not care he is dead."

Carla gave Maria's shoulder a sympathetic squeeze. How sad that the family was in disarray instead of supporting each other. More than once, she and Owen had been touched by the affection and closeness of families in Portugal. Teenage boys kissed their grandmothers. Mothers always seemed to be hugging their children or smoothing back their hair. Babies in strollers were the kings and queens of the plaza. Obviously, Maria's wasn't one of those families.

"People handle grief in different ways," Carla said tactfully.

"There is no grief in my aunt. My cousins know this, too. There was no love in their house. They would say this to my mother when they visited us. Before they went away to get work. It is for that they have stayed away." Maria lifted a palm. "Assim é a vida."

"Mmm," Carla murmured, hearing the familiar phrase.

"So now we will find out why Senhora Gonzaga lied." Maria's voice took on a flinty tone. "She has never liked me."

Carla blinked her surprise. Senhora Gonzaga had made it sound as if they'd never even spoken. "Did she tell you that?"

"No, but I can see from her eyes when she looks at me. If I say 'boa tarde' or 'bom dia,' she will only nod. When I pay, she never says 'obrigada.' And she never smiles at me."

Yeah. That's probably a good sign.

Carla glanced across the street and nearly groaned. Across from them, on the corner, Tiffany-from-Nevada's thin figure pivoted in what looked like hesitation. For a moment, she seemed to be about to start down toward Senhora Gonzaga's café. Looking around, she spotted Carla and hurried across the street instead, cheerfully waving.

Now, of all times! Carla closed her eyes, then opened them, bracing for Tiffany's energy.

Today Tiffany wore flowered ballet flats, white Capris and a three-quarter sleeve T-shirt with lace trim. *And those awful sunglasses.* "You were so right about those gardens," she gushed, as she came up to them. "Jeez, I musta taken a million pics. Wanna see?" She started to unzip the camera bag around her neck.

Carla forced a little laugh. "I've probably taken the same pictures myself."

"Of course." Tiffany slapped her forehead. "What am I thinking!" Her glance took in Maria who was staring at the square stones of the walk.

"Your friend doesn't like Portugal?" Tiffany asked. "She doesn't look too thrilled."

"She's from here," Carla said impatiently. "She has a lot on her mind."

"Oh. Sorry."

A twinge of guilt for her abruptness made Carla add, "I'm sure your friends in Reno will love to see your pictures."

"For sure! This place is unbelievable." Tiffany looked at the gift shop's doorway. "Gosh, they're open. What luck! I need to pick up some souvenirs."

"It's a nice shop," Carla assured her. "Enjoy the rest of your stay in Braga." She stretched her mouth in a false smile and took Maria's elbow.

As they started across the street, she said in a low voice, "Remember, we're only visiting Senhora Gonzaga because we know she lied, and we want the truth, so that Paulo isn't found guilty of killing your uncle." Thinking of Maria's quarrelsome family, she added, "We shouldn't get angry with her or have words."

"Have words?"

"Let's not get into an argument with her. We just want her to tell us what she really saw and to clear Paulo of what he didn't do. He's already in enough trouble for what he did do."

The two salmon-colored umbrellas above the outside tables had already been unfurled, their warm tones the perfect complement to the deep green of the leaf-laden linden trees lining the street.

"I'm the one Rosa talked to yesterday, so let me do the talking," Carla said. "Just steer the conversation back to English if Senhora Gonzaga starts talking in Portuguese, okay?"

It was only a few minutes after nine. The café wouldn't be too busy yet. A good time to talk. Then she'd call Detetive Fernandes. How satisfying it would be to tell him the first witness who implicated Paulo was unreliable.

Carla noticed the large door to the right of the café. Probably to the flat upstairs, the one with the geraniums on the balcony. Maybe Senhora Gonzaga lived above her café the way Natália and her husband lived above the barber shop.

There was no sign of Rosa when they entered. Senhora Gonzaga had just given a small cup of espresso to the sole customer, a man in a green work suit at a table near the far wall. As he downed a large sip, the proprietress eyed them warily, hands clasped in front of her yellow bib apron, the sleeves of a gray and white print blouse ending below the elbow with a tasteful ruffle.

Her gaze shifted from Carla to Maria, and back to Carla. "Bom dia." she said. "Please sit. I will be right with you.*"*

"Actually, we need to talk to you." Carla looked around. She had counted on Rosa being there to take care of customers and, if necessary, to back up her claim that Senhora Gonzaga had gone to O Belo's when she claimed to be in the café. "Where's your helper?" she asked.

"She cannot come in today. She have twist her uncle." Carla's confusion must have shown on her face. The proprietress pointed to her foot.

Ah. Ankle.

Senhora Gonzaga walked over to them, her forehead drawn in concern. "What you want to talk about?"

Carla took a deep breath. In a low voice, in case the customer understood English, she said, "Why did you tell the police—and me—that you saw Paulo go into the wine shop and stay for a long time when Senhor Costa was killed?"

Senhora Gonzaga's stare was like a prim reprimand. "Paulo? Who is this Paulo?"

Maria bristled. "You know who Paulo is!"

"He's the young man you told the police you saw," Carla said. "The 'chico.'"

"Please to excuse me." Senhora Gonzaga went behind the counter as the customer came to the register to pay for his drink.

As soon as he left, Maria launched into rapid Portuguese.

"Keep me in the loop," Carla said. "What did you just tell her?"

"I said she made much trouble for Paulo. I ask why she lies."

Carla blew her breath out. *So much for 'let me do the talking.'*

"But he *was* in shop. I see him," Senhora Gonzaga told Carla.

"You couldn't know how long, though." Carla said. "You went to look at O Belo's shoe sale and couldn't find what you wanted. Rosa took over the customers for you for maybe half an hour, but you told the police you were here all that time."

"You have question my waitress?" An affronted look came over Senhora Gonzaga's face. "What is your interest in this, Senhora Bass?"

Carla met her gaze. "*I* found the body. *I* made the report. And ever since then, people have been after me. I've been threatened. A man tried to kill me." She felt her ire mount. "If *you* hadn't given false information, the case might be settled by now. I won't feel safe until it is settled, so I need you to start telling the truth."

"I am sorry you have so much trouble," Senhora Gonzaga murmured, and for a moment she did look sorry. Sad even. Then, "But I do not have to tell you why I do anything. You are not police."

"You need to tell the police, then. Or I will. You're a likely suspect, you know," Carla added. "You could have gone to Costa's shop instead of to O Belo's." For a moment, she wondered again if the proprietress really was the culprit. Then she re-ran the logistics through her mind: too long and involved a route, given the time frame Rosa had mentioned. *Thirty minutes* wouldn't *work. It's Vitore or O Lobo.*

"You probably don't realize how much trouble you've made for Paulo," she said, softening her tone.

Senhora Gonzaga pinched her lips together and frowned, as if coming to a decision. "Come, we will talk about this privately. Please, sit," she said again, nodding at the table where her customer had sat. She came around the counter, walked to the glass door, turned the sign on the door so that "Fechada" faced out, then twisted the deadbolt.

"Is private, between us," she explained. "No customers to interrupt."

Carla hesitated, then decided that made sense. She had wanted a private conversation in the first place, which was why she had originally envisioned going outside while Rosa took care of customers inside. With a nod to Maria, she took a window table instead of the one in the corner, and pulled out a chair on one side. She sat, staring through the clear pane below the cafe's name at the wine shop across the street, trying to imagine exactly how much would have been visible to Senhora Gonzaga on Monday.

But Senhora Gonzaga probably would have been at the cash register, she reminded herself. *If she was in the shop. When she was in the shop. Rosa would have been with customers.*

Maria took the chair next to Carla. She scowled at the proprietress, who started toward them from the doorway, then halted.

"Ah não! Is the Americana again!" A hand went to her temple. Carla followed her gaze out the window and saw Tiffany crossing at the corner to their side of the cobbled street.

"Always she bothering me! Every day," Senhora Gonzaga said in an aggrieved tone. "Two times she come

217

yesterday. Always to ask so many questions. She is worse than you, senhora. Want to know everything about Braga. 'If you want to know so much,' I tell her, 'why you don't buy guide book? Go to Turismo office.' But no. Is for her Portuguese background." Senhora Gonzaga's palm shot up and she gave a disgusted blink that involved a quick head tilt as well. Carla had to admire the expressiveness of Portuguese body language. She scrutinized Tiffany, who was nearing the door.

Glitzy. Ditzy. Probably grew up watching reality shows.

"She want to know names," the proprietress grumbled. "Who live here? Who work here? Because her mother's grandmother was from here."

"From Braga?" Carla asked.

"Sim."

Yeah, that figures. Two generations of fitting into American culture. Then maybe Tiffany's mother had a revived interest in ancestry, leading to Tiffany's Braga trip.

Tiffany rapped on the glass, apparently oblivious to the sign, and Senhora Gonzaga marched to the door.

"Fechada," she said loudly.

"I don't speak Portuguese," Tiffany whined. Her huge sunglasses slid forward on her thin nose and she pushed them back.

"Café is not open. I have bad headache," Senhora Gonzaga said.

Tiffany pointed through the plate glass window. "You let them in."

"Is my niece and her friend."

Carla exchanged a wry glance with Maria before returning her attention to Tiffany, who was studying them. It was hard to read her expression behind the garish sunglasses.

"I left my wallet here," Tiffany called. "I need it."

"You don't leave no wallet here," Senhora Gonzaga said loudly. "Maybe is at your hotel. Call this boyfriend you tell me about!"

"Oh. That's possible. Okay. Yeah. I'll check." Tiffany started punching numbers into a cell phone she took from her handbag, then turned her back for what seemed to be an involved conversation, her free hand gesticulating. When she turned around again, her shoulders slumped.

"It's not there. It had all my money. All my credit cards."

Remembering her own sick feeling when her purse was taken yesterday, Carla felt a surge of sympathy.

Wait a minute! Wasn't Tiffany at the gift shop a few minutes ago, buying souvenirs?

"Is not my problem," Senhora Gonzaga called. "You should report to police."

"Good idea. I'm sorry I bothered you."

"Sorry. You always sorry you bother me," Senhora Gonzaga muttered, turning her back on Tiffany, who was punching phone buttons again.

"She have no shame, that one," the proprietress told Carla and Maria, jerking a thumb toward the door. "She travel with her namorado, and they are not marry."

Her face drew up in a remorseful expression. "And now I am sorry for bad temper. I *do* have headache. Come, we will go upstairs. I make fresh café for you. We talk and no one to disturb us." She motioned with her chin toward a door that led, Carla realized, to the entry hall of the entrance she'd seen outside.

So, she does live over the café. Still, the café's access to the building's entrance was a surprise.

"Come," Senhora Gonzaga prodded, "and I tell you what you want to know." She brushed past them and opened the door, managing to look almost chic despite the fact she still wore her apron.

Carla rose. Maria followed suit. Carla slid another quick look at Tiffany, who was walking back and forth, phone to her ear, nodding while chewing at a fingernail.

She could *have lost her wallet yesterday. And only discovered it missing at the gift shop a few minutes ago.* Tiffany didn't look like the organized type. Satisfied on that point, Carla half-nodded to Maria. They followed Senhora Gonzaga into the entry hall where dim light filtered from the window in the front door, their steps echoing across the black-and-white marble floor.

"When my husband buy this building," Senhora Gonzaga told them, "he have the café door put in. In rain, you don't have to go out. He think of smart things like that."

"He sounds like a wonderful man," Carla murmured, since nothing else came to mind.

"But he die and leave me alone." Senhora Gonzaga's voice was heavy with resentment.

Over her shoulder, Carla grimaced at Maria. "What a sourpuss," she mouthed, and then realized "sourpuss" probably wasn't a familiar term to Maria.

As they followed the proprietress up the remaining stairs, Carla was reminded of mysteries where the victim had gone either upstairs or downstairs and met a poor fate. A shudder ran through her. She willed it away. Owen was right.

She *did* read too many mysteries. Besides, Maria was with her. They were two against one.

And Maria has her ankle knife. That last thought, reassuring as should have been, gave Carla a new shudder. *Don't be melodramatic,* she reprimanded herself. *We're here to find out why Senhora Gonzaga lied about Paulo and what she actually saw.*

The proprietress unlocked the door on her left.

"Please to come in," she said with a smile.

Chapter Twenty-Six –Because of Family

They entered directly into the sala de estar. Senhora Gonzaga closed the door behind them, twisting the lock with a little click that made Carla uneasy again. But then, she and Owen always locked the door to their apartment here, too. Braga had a low crime rate, but it was a city, after all, and city habits died hard. They always locked their doors in Piedmont.

Carla took in the décor: Nubby, beige fabric on sofa and chairs to the right. Orange-and-black print throw pillows that accented salmon walls. A dark, rectangular coffee table with a glass top. Two matching end tables.

But the entertainment center across the room spoils the effect, kiddo. Dark wood shelves flanked a large, flat wall TV and held plaster statues of what she took to be saints, along with a vase of yellow and white plastic daisies, stacks of magazines, and a few newspapers that were clearly tabloids. A bulky black purse sprawled on the tabloids like a gigantic paperweight. Overhead, an inexpensive globe lampshade hugged the ceiling.

The dining table and four chairs by the window looked like they might be of ebony. *That could be veneer.* Dingy, beige carpeting covered the floor. The designer in Carla wanted to revamp the whole room. Politely, she said, "You have an interesting flat."

The proprietress only said, for the third time, "Please sit." She motioned with a hand toward the sofa, but Carla walked over to the dinette set by the window, peering out at the geranium-filled, wrought- iron balcony. Across the street, the blue-and-white tiled facade of Costa's shop gleamed in the morning sun. She hadn't bothered to notice the brickwork above it before. The curtained windows suggested an apartment. Now she wondered if Costa, like Senhora Gonzaga, had lived above his place of business, away from his estranged wife.

"Please sit," Senhora Gonzaga insisted. "I will make café."

Carla turned from the window and pulled out a chair, hanging her handbag on its back. *No danger of someone stealing it here.* She tilted her head, appraising the opposite wall. A framed print of white and pink roses in a blue vase hung crookedly next to the door Senhora Gonzaga exited. Resisting an urge to get up and go straighten the print, Carla propped her elbows on the table, hands folded against her chin.

Maria took the end chair facing the hall door, and they waited. A round clock on the wall near the same door ticked loudly. Despite the Roman Numerals on its face, Carla doubted it was an antique. She wound her wristwatch for something to do. *Already 9:30.* As if to confirm that, church bells chimed the half hour. Maria fidgeted with her purse strap, but whispered, "It is good she has invited us for café in her home. Here she will be comfortable, and she will listen to us."

Carla nodded. Hospitality had a way of smoothing the rough edges of the most difficult conversations. That was true in business. Hopefully it was true now.

223

"I should not have spoken angrily to her," Maria admitted.

"She'll understand," Carla said. "You've lost your uncle. You're upset about your boyfriend."

Senhora Gonzaga returned, carrying a tray with three small cups of espresso on saucers, a sugar bowl, and a plate of biscoitos—those twisty butter cookies with a tang of orange that made it almost impossible for Carla to eat only one. Inadvertently, Carla licked her lips.

The proprietress smiled at her. "I see you like these, yes? I make them yesterday, but they are just like fresh." She gave each of them napkins for the cookies and sat across from Carla. Once they were quietly sipping and munching, a pleasant feeling of warmth filled the room.

Maria shared her mother's recipe for biscoitos with Senhora Gonzaga, then translated for Carla. "The secret is to knead the dough well," she said, and rubbed her fingers against her palms for demonstration.

Senhora Gonzaga nodded vigorously, smiling. "Sim." Then, as if a switch had been flicked, her smile faded. Abruptly, she put everything back on the tray and took things back to the kitchen, returning a moment later.

When she sat again, her face was devoid of cheer. Leaning forward, hands flat on the table, she said, "Now we talk. What you want to know?"

Maria said something in Portuguese and Senhora Gonzaga gave a stiff, "Obrigada," but some inner thought made her lips bunch together.

"I apologized to her for my anger," Maria explained to Carla.

Good girl! Although the senhora could *be a little more gracious about it.*

224

The proprietress turned to Carla. "What you want to know?" she repeated.

"Please, Senhora Gonzaga, tell us what you saw Monday," Carla said. "It will help the police find the real culprit, and I want to get on with my life."

"Your life," the proprietress murmured after a moment. "What of my life?"

Excuse me?

At that, Maria leaned forward, her face wiped clean of apology, and said something in Portuguese. To Carla, she said, "I told her this is not about her life. It is about Paulo's."

Hey! My life, too, kiddo!

"Yes, we must speak English for your friend!" Senhora Gonzaga said. Her voice had turned raspy. "Your friend who is so much curious. You really should not be so curious, Senhora Bass." The woman's eyes glittered with dislike, as if the earlier warmth had been carried out on the tray with the cups and cookies. Carla was taken aback.

Senhora Gonzaga glowered at Maria. "Is your fault."

Maria frowned. "What is my fault?"

"Your uncle saves money so we can go to Brazil, because your aunt will not divorce him. 'We go to Brazil and start new life,' he tells me. 'No one will know we are not marry.'" She closed her eyes and heaved a deep sigh. "For three years, I believe him."

Carla lifted her brows, remembering Senhora Gonzaga's earlier comment about Tiffany being shameless because she was traveling with a boyfriend. *Different rules, apparently.*

"You are . . . his . . . his," Maria stuttered, "his woman."

Senhora Gonzaga lifted her head, staring at Maria as a queen might regard a peon. Maria lowered her eyes. When she looked up again, the expression in her eyes was fathomless. "What happened?" she asked. "Why didn't you go to Brazil?"

"Because of you!" The ferocity in Senhora Gonzaga's voice raised the hairs on Carla's neck.

Maria flinched. "I don't understand."

"You visit his shop. And then he start worry about your chico." She looked at Carla. "People tell him they see her with a namorado, and he learns it is the same chico who is asking too many questions of him. Roberto don't tell me what questions, but he says this chico is bad man and bad for her. He will make her forget her studies. You see, her mother have told Roberto her studies is so important." Senhora Gonzaga's lip curled.

Maria's face flushed. "Paulo was never a problem for my studies," she said heatedly. "Is that why you want to get him in trouble?"

Wondering where all of this was going, Carla made her tone soothing as she asked, "What does this have to do with what you brought us upstairs to talk about?"

Senhora Gonzaga took a small candy with metallic wrapping from her apron pocket. Carla froze, watching her unwrap the toffee and pop it into her mouth, then crinkle the paper in her fingers.

"You see," Senhora Gonzaga said, and Carla stiffened. She was going to hear a confession. In every mystery she had read, confessions didn't bode well for listeners.

Senhora Gonzaga let the wrapper fall to the floor. Her face puckered as if she were about to cry. "Segunda . . .

Monday, he call me at the café. He tell me to meet him after work, because things have change. 'What kind of things?' I ask him. 'Change how?' But he don't say. I tell Rosa to look after the café while I go to the shoe sale. Just a quick look, I say. I go to his wine shop instead.

"From the gate on the other side," Carla murmured. "Into the corridor." Still, how did she go so quickly?

"There is patio between shops," Senhora Gonzaga told Maria. "Your friend here knows this. She ask me about it Monday." The glance she threw Carla radiated ill will.

"Why didn't Rosa see you cross the street?" Carla asked.

"I send her to get more plates from storage room and to check refrigerator before I leave, and then I walk to Rua de São Gonçalves instead of Rua dos Chãos and come around on street behind Roberto's shop.

Carla nodded. The trip she had imagined, minus the detour to Avenida Central. It probably saved the proprietress nearly ten minutes each way. On return, it wouldn't be hard to see through the glass door where Rosa was standing and then enter when her back was turned.

"I go into his office from patio," Senhora Gonzaga said. "I hear you in shop, senhora, paying for your Port. I wait in office for you to leave. Then I come into shop. I tell him, 'What kind of things have change we must talk?' But I already know.

"'We cannot talk now,' he tells me. 'The Americana will come back. I gave her something she will return when she finds out.'"

Senhora Gonzaga fingered the bib of her apron, her mouth twisted in a bitter smile. "You see, he is like that. He figure people out, how to use them. He use me, but I don't

227

know that for so long time. He make promises, but he only like having affair."

"What did he want to talk about?" Carla asked, the dull weight in her stomach telling her she already knew. *No more Brazil.*

Senhora Gonzaga made a snorting sound, as if disgusted. "He say we cannot go away like we plan. He don't love his wife, but he cannot do such thing to his children or his niece!" She fairly shouted "niece". "As if his sons care about him! As if—"

"His sons do care about him," Maria said. "It is their mother they find . . . difficult."

"But *you!*" Senhora Gonzaga snarled. "He say you don't have no one to look after you in Braga if he is not here. The other uncles have die or move to other countries. 'Family comes first,' he tells me. But what about me, e? What about me?"

"I should have visited him more," Maria said in a low voice. Her eyes were wet.

"He was probably happy you visited him as much as you did," Carla murmured.

"Yes! Comfort her!" Senhora Gonzaga's voice was full of spite. "But who is there to comfort me? I don't have family. My husband and I were not bless with children. When my husband die, Roberto comfort me. He was all I have." She held a clenched fist to her mouth and closed her eyes.

"What happened?" Carla asked softly.

"He tell me, 'We still go on as before.' He try to . . . to hold me, but I push him away, I am so angry. I push him hard, and he falls." Senhora Gonzaga burst into tears. "I have killed him," she sobbed.

"It was an accident," Carla said, and the relief sweeping over her that she wasn't dealing with a cold-blooded murderess made her almost giddy. "You have to go to the police and tell them how it happened." She searched through her handbag for her pack of tissues. Finding it, she handed it to Senhora Gonzaga. "They won't consider it murder. I'm sure you'll be treated fairly."

Senhora Gonzaga ignored her outstretched hand. "My café will fail. My husband and I start it so many years ago, and it will be ruin. No one will come again ever." She swiped at the tears on her cheek with the back of her hand. "No, senhora, I cannot do that.

"And you, Maria," she said, "I am sorry you worry about this Paulo. He is not good for you, but I understand how a man make you foolish." Getting up, Senhora Gonzaga walked over to the huge purse that was sitting on the tabloids and brought it back to the table. She put it on the table, then unsnapped it, peering into it a moment.

A gun! Carla felt her forehead turn suddenly damp with perspiration. *Don't go up those stairs. Don't go into the spider's web. Don't* . . . She shot a quick glance at Maria, who looked equally alarmed.

But Senhora Gonzaga only took out a compact, then a tube of lipstick, which she carefully applied to her lips, smoothing the soft color with her little finger. "Is shame," she said, and gave an odd laugh. "When I eat biscoitos, I eat lipstick, too." She took out a tissue and dabbed at her wet cheeks, regarding herself in the compact mirror for a long moment before putting it back in her purse.

"Bem," she said softly, and she hung the oversized purse on the back of her chair. As if just realizing she still wore her apron, she untied the strings behind her neck and took it off, hanging it next to her purse. "I am forgetting," she told them. "We are not in café downstairs."

Now that the proprietress seemed calm again, Carla saw her chance. 'If you explain to the police that it was an accident," she began.

"I tell the police *nothing*," the proprietress said in a voice that made Carla wonder how she ever saw this woman as soft. "I will wait. And then I will sell the Manoel Beleza de Andrade Port." She laughed again, a loud laugh this time that sounded half strangled.

"The bottle that was in the case?" Carla sat back, trying to wrap her head around what the proprietress had just said. "The 1812 bottle?" New realization seeped into her mind like a stain. *The welt on his forehead. He didn't die when he fell.*

A knowing look came into Senhora Gonzaga's eyes, as if she read Carla's mind.

"You are too smart for your own good, Senhora," she said. "I see you know. It was not accident. I came to kill him. When he fall, I hear him moan. I smash the case and take the bottle, and I hit him hard to make sure. And then he is quiet."

Into the stunned silence that followed, she took a deep breath, looking from one to the other. "I am sorry, but you both must have accident."

Chapter Twenty-Seven – The Best Laid Plans

Carla closed her eyes. *After serving cookies? After applying make-up? Really?* She opened her eyes again and saw Senhora Gonzaga's wild expression. *Yeah. Really.*

Maria squared her shoulders. "There are two of us, and only one of you."

"Is no matter."

"And I have this!" Maria reached down, rolled up her cuff, and whipped out the small, thin knife she had shown Carla at the museum. "There will be no accident," she said to Senhora Gonzaga, then broke into Portuguese.

To Carla, Maria said, "I have told her she must come with us to the police."

She fixed her gaze on Senhora Gonzaga again. "I know how to use this."

The older woman took a small, snub-nosed revolver from her pocket. "And I know how to use *this*. Is my husband's," she added, as if that information might interest them.

In the ensuing silence, Carla thought of the cliché that in moments like this your heart stops beating. Hers kept right on going. She could feel the pulse beating away in her throat and ears. She could hear it, too—*ka-thunk, ka-thunk, ka-thunk.*

231

"You can't shoot us," she heard herself say in a calm voice that surely must be someone else's. "How will you explain it to the police?"

"Yes, I am thinking about this in the kitchen when I make café. Roberto's niece is crazy from her uncle death. She comes to my home while you and I are having conversation."

"Why?" asked Carla in as calm a voice as she could muster. "Why would she come?" *Keep her talking.*

"Because I get her boyfriend in trouble with police for kill her uncle. She try to attack me and I shoot." Eyeing Maria's knife, she smirked. "You making it easy for me."

"You'd better put it down," Carla said to Maria.

After a moment's hesitation, Maria laid the knife on the table.

"Won't shooting her be worse than killing Senhor Costa by accident?" Carla asked.

"No. Because I defend myself. Nobody know about Roberto and me. Nobody will."

Senhor Torres seemed to. Should I say that?

"What about me?" Carla asked instead.

"You try to help me, but you get in way."

Great. "What are we supposed to be having our conversation about?"

Senhora Gonzaga pursed her lips. "Maybe you are coming here to ask me to teach you Portuguese." She laughed a mirthless laugh.

"Do you really think I would tell them that?" Carla asked.

"You don't say nothing. Is so sad. You try to defend me from this crazy girl, and my gun go off. I can make story they believe!"

After O Lobo had grabbed her throat, Carla had thought nothing could ever scare her so much again. She was right. Instead of fear, she felt a slow, steady anger building. This pathetic woman who might have aroused sympathy was willing to kill two innocent people because her affair hadn't worked out? Because she had killed him in a fit of anger or jealousy or whatever? Because she had messed up? *And I'm supposed to be okay with that?*

"You mean . . . like I was trying to push you away from her?" Carla asked.

"Sim," Senhora Gonzaga nodded eagerly. "Like that."

"Away from her knife, right?"

Senhora Gonzaga frowned, as if perplexed by Carla's willingness to help her alibi.

"I don't think that will work." Carla pushed her chair back and stood up.

Senhora Gonzaga rose, too, her knuckles turning white as she tightened her grasp on the gun. Anxiety had wiped the sneer off her face. "Sit down, senhora."

Instead, Carla turned, walked past Maria, and marched over to the far wall, picking up the vase with plastic daisies and examining it. "My back is to you," she said over her shoulder. "I don't think you can convince the police I got in the way of the bullet you meant for Maria."

"Come back and sit down," Senhora Gonzaga's voice trembled.

"And for another thing," Carla said. "I'm way over here. Maria's way over there. Your bullets will be all at the wrong angles." She hoped that was true. In the mysteries she read, angles sounded important.

"You will come here!" Senhora Gonzaga's voice was closer. If Carla could get her past Maria, Maria could jump her from behind.

"Come and get me," Carla said.

A moment later, she felt Senhora Gonzaga's hand on her arm, surprisingly strong. As the proprietress spun her around, Carla grabbed her wrist and shoved her arm toward the ceiling, dropping the vase to get a good hold with both hands. For good measure, she kicked Senhora Gonzaga. The force of it made her right shoe come off, but the proprietress merely cursed in Portuguese and hung on to the revolver, her finger on the trigger as they stumbled across the rug. The crash of the vase was accompanied by the crack of a bullet from the revolver and tinkling shards of glass from the shattered lamp overhead. From somewhere else, Carla heard the sound of more breaking glass. Something huge, from the smash and crash of it. She tightened her hold on Senhora Gonzaga's wrist.

Maria came from behind, grabbing Senhora Gonzaga's hand, but still the woman wouldn't let go and yanked her arm free. The gun went off again. This time the print on the far wall shattered. Carla lunged, and the three of them went down, scuffling on the dingy rug. She tried to pry Senhora Gonzaga's fingers loose, but the proprietress thrashed from side to side, her legs kicking, while her free hand scrabbled until she managed to grab Carla's hair and pull hard.

"Damn!" Carla nearly let go at the painful yank. Luckily, Maria had a good grasp on Senhora Gonzaga's wrist. Carla tightened her own handhold, grimacing from the pain in her scalp. Maria banged Senhora Gonzaga's hand against the floor. Still holding the gun, the woman let loose a stream of Portuguese that sounded like pure invective. She let go of Carla's hair with her free hand and reached for Maria's throat. Carla elbowed her in the stomach, while Maria managed to kneel on the woman's other arm, grinding her weight into her elbow.

"*Ai!*"

"Let go," Carla said, through panted breaths. All of them were panting, she realized. Senhora Gonzaga had finally stopped struggling, but Carla was afraid to let her up, since she still hung onto the gun. And now there was a rattle of a door knob, a loud thump against the hall door, another thump—a kicking kind of thump, Carla thought dizzily, followed by the splintering crash of wood.

A moment later, a flowered ballet flat came down on Senhora Gonzaga's hand.

"Ai!" Senhora Gonzaga cried again, and her fingers loosened. Pointing her own gun at the woman, Tiffany, no longer wearing sunglasses, reached over and picked up Senhora Gonzaga's revolver. A stray piece of glass fell from her sleeve.

Tiffany? An undercover agent? Working for the Braga police? Without her sunglasses, she looked a little older than Carla had pegged her for. Late twenties, maybe. Her large, expressive brown eyes and regretful half-smile seemed at odds with the two guns she held.

Fernandes quietly walked in through the remains of the door, followed by Chefe Esteves, both holding Berettas. Esteves turned, twisted the lock, and opened the broken door wide to allow Agente Cunha to walk comfortably through. Esteves brushed a fragment of glass from his lapel.

A surreal image popped into Carla's mind of a gesticulating crowd gathering outside the café's shattered plate glass window . . . Torres holding his palms out, explaining, "You see . . ."

Get a grip, Carla.

She pushed herself off the proprietress, scrambled to her feet, one shoe on, one shoe off, and smoothed her skirt. She ran her fingers through her hair, wincing, and noticed a few blonde hairs in her would-be killer's hand. Fernandes helped Senhora Gonzaga to her feet and Esteves handcuffed her. Tiffany pocketed her own gun, handing Senhora Gonzaga's to Fernandes.

All the fight had gone out of the proprietress. One sleeve was torn. Her bun had come undone, and her hair lay in gray-streaked waves over her shoulders. Her mouth drooped at the corners. Despite that, Carla could see she once had been pretty. For a moment, she felt sad for the woman until she flashed on the snub-nosed revolver Gonzaga had trained on her and Maria.

"What took you so long," she asked Fernandes. "Why didn't you just—I don't know—shoot the lock off the door?"

He lifted his brows. "And perhaps hit one of you, if you were by the door? We don't like to shoot the wrong person."

Carla took a deep breath. "No. Of course not." She spied her shoe near an end table and hobbled over to it. When she looked up again, he was eyeing her.

"Any injuries?" he asked.

She shook her head. "Not really. My scalp stings a little. That's about it."

"By the way," he added, "your friend Paulo finally turned himself in."

"Really?" she asked, slipping on the shoe. "Will that help him at this late date?"

Fernandes lifted his shoulders. "It might." He turned his attention to the sofa, where Agent Esteves had led Senhora Gonzaga. Her cuffed hands in her lap, she rocked back and forth, weeping.

Cunha went through the bedroom door, then came back quickly, walking over to Fernandes. He muttered something in a low tone.

Maria had retrieved her knife from the table. She sat and rolled up her jeans cuff, returning the knife to its ankle sheath, which elicited a sharp question from Tiffany in Portuguese.

"Não," Maria said. "She asked me if it was a switchblade," she explained to Carla, "They are illegal."

"Wait." Carla stared at Tiffany. "You speak Portuguese?"

Tiffany looked amused. "Sure."

"But you're from Reno."

"I've never been outside of Portugal in my life."

"And your name probably isn't Tiffany."

"Nope."

"You sound so authentic," Carla marveled. "No accent at all. How . . .?"

Tiffany-who-was-not-Tiffany laughed. "Television. I've watched American programs ever since I was a kid. I love American TV."

Maria stood up, her bag slung over her shoulder. "You fooled even me."

Senhora Gonzaga rubbed her shin and unloosed a new stream of Portuguese Carla was sure she didn't want to understand.

"You kicked her?" Fernandes asked. "You seem to find ever new uses for shoes."

Esteves helped the proprietress to her feet and led her out the door, no doubt to a police car waiting below.

Detetive Fernandes gave the woman Carla now thought of as Not-Tiffany a nod. "Bem feito," he said, which Carla decided was a congratulation. "A team is coming to collect more evidence," he added. "I understand there is a rare 1812 Port in Senhora Gonzaga's bedroom."

"Sorry if I complicated things," Carla told him.

He shrugged. "There are always complications. It worked to our advantage."

Her contrition vanished. She turned to Not-Tiffany.

"What made you sure Senhora Gonzaga was the one who killed Costa?"

"Fingerprints."

"Fingerprints!" Carla thought back to her phone conversation with Fernandes, when he had said matching prints on the wrappers were only useful if the same prints were already in the system. "So Senhora Gonzaga has a record?"

"The prints on a spoon matched the ones on both wrappers," said the agent. "The spoon Senhora Gonzaga handled when I ordered coffee yesterday afternoon. You might say you inspired me when you took Senhor Vitore's spoon."

"When I took . . . what!" Carla put her hands on her hips. "You're the one who stole my purse."

Not-Tiffany looked pained. "'Stole' is a harsh word. You could say I relieved you of the chore of delivering it." She grinned at Fernandes, who returned the barest hint of a smile.

To Carla he said, "Agente Alcides downstairs will take you and Senhorita Santos home."

"My aunt's house is in the hills," Maria protested. "I can take a bus."

"It is no problem for Agente Alcides to take you," Fernandes said firmly. "He can drop Senhora Bass off first."

"Yes, please!" Carla nodded. Time to pull herself together before meeting Owen for lunch. A cup of coffee. A hot bath. A change of clothes. Carla checked her watch and blinked—not even ten-thirty! How could so much have happened in such a short time? *And just how am I going to explain all of this to Owen?*

"After lunch, I would appreciate it if you both return to the station to give your testimony," Fernandes told Carla and Maria.

So there goes the trip to Bom Jesus.

"I will be glad to testify against this woman," said Maria. "My cousins can bring me."

"Okay," Carla said. *As if I can refuse.* A wave of resentment welled in her. She was tired of being at the mercy of everyone else's decisions. This week she'd been tricked by Costa, half-throttled by O Lobo, given ominous messages to deliver from Geoffrey Walsh, semi-stalked by Vitore, had her arm yanked by Senhora Gonzaga—who also pulled her hair and, more importantly, pulled a gun on her. She'd been told by Fernandes to spy on Maria, then to keep out of things. He had told her not to leave the country until . . ..

Carla's thoughts came to an abrupt halt. She smiled at Fernandes.

"What?" he asked, when she didn't say anything.

"So. Detetive Fernandes, can I assume I'm no longer a suspect?"

Chapter Twenty-Eight – All's Well
That Ends Well—for Some

At the end of their Monday Skype call, Carla told Bethany, "Now that I'm a free woman, let's plan for Jessica to set up appointments sometime soon with Mrs. Weatherby and the Duartes. I'd like to see their houses. I'd like to see Mrs. Demming again, too. It'll be nice to actually see the Da Silva Porto paintings on her walls."

"Stay for a week," Bethany suggested, scribbling on a notepad. "You can stay at my place a couple of nights and we can go hang out and do girl talk."

"Nothing before next week, though, okay? Owen and I are going to Ponte de Lima next week-end."

"Got it," Bethany said. "So . . . details, please."

"About Ponte de Lima?" Carla teased. "Lots of old buildings, lots of azulejo tiles, from the pictures. And there's a platoon of Roman soldier statues on one of the banks. It goes with a legend about the river."

"You know what I mean," Bethany said. "The case."

"The case." Carla rubbed her eyes. "Long story."

Bethany tapped her pen against her desk. "I hope I'm not going to have to wait a couple of weeks or so to hear it."

"It really is a long story," Carla said. She ran her fingers through a lock of hair—the spot where Senhora Gonzaga had yanked—and winced.

There had been the trip to the police station where Carla and Maria gave their testimony while Owen and one of

240

Maria's cousins—a handsome young man who resembled Maria—waited. Afterward, Detetive Fernandes had taken all of them into another room and offered them soft drinks from a vending machine.

"Things turned out well," Fernandes told Carla. "You and Senhorita Costa both were lucky. It seems to me I'm always telling you that," he added, lacing his fingers, tapping his thumbs together, his pale gaze severe.

"What's going to happen to Vitore and O Lobo? Have they said who the forger is?" she asked.

Owen said, "Carla . . .."

Ignoring him, she had coaxed, "C'mon, detective. You owe me that much. I did get a confession out of Senhora Gonzaga."

"The café owner killed Costa," she told Bethany now. "He was going to dump her, and she lost it. She shoved him way too hard. And then she bonked him with a wine bottle to make sure he was dead."

"She told you all this? Killers don't share stuff like that."

"Yeah, well. She pulled a gun on me and Maria. She's going to be prosecuted for his death and for trying to kill us." Not-Tiffany had told her that much. In the station, Senhora Gonzaga had broken down in further tears and confessed the whole story again to Fernandes.

"This woman pulled a gun on you?" Bethany's voice went shrill. Her eyes seemed to double in size. "How's Owen handling all this? He can't be too happy."

"You're right about that. He's gone from being upset to relieved, to upset again."

"Duh. Two people have tried to kill you in the space of a week! I was worried sick about you when you hung up

241

Friday. I knew you were going to do something you shouldn't."

"Two people *threatened* to kill me," Carla corrected.

"And came pretty close to succeeding, if you ask me."

Carla didn't answer, remembering Owen's distraught face. "I'm just glad everything turned out okay, and they caught her," Bethany said.

"Yeah, but only because she made two mistakes."

"There you go, all sleuth-y again! What mistakes?"

"One," Carla ticked off on her finger, "she shouldn't have tried to pin the death on Paulo. If she had never lied, it still would seem more likely O Lobo or his boss did it. No one would suspect her. Of course, she wouldn't know that. But, two, she really didn't have to confess to Maria and me that she was the one who killed Costa."

"You kinda forced her hand."

Carla pursed her lips. "That's what Owen said."

"So, what happens now with this Paulo?"

"He's off the hook for murder. But he'll face prosecution for theft. O Lobo admitted Paulo was only involved in the bottle switch. He's willing to testify Vitore planned the swindle."

"Vitore?"

"The vintner who set up the whole thing. And *he'll* face prosecution for *that* part." Over cups of coffee in Carla's kitchen Sunday—Owen had driven off somewhere to brood alone—Natália had translated the front story of Vitore's arrest in *O Examinador.*

"Ah, the company you keep!" Bethany said.

Carla attempted a smile. "Just another episode in the life of an interior decorator abroad."

"I hope there won't be any more like that, honey."

242

"You and me both. Not to mention Owen." Carla brightened. "We're eating out tonight." At noon he had called her, apparently in relieved mode again, saying she needed a restful evening that would take her mind off everything. That was when he had also suggested the Ponte de Lima trip.

Bethany propped her chin on her hands. "Your friend Maria must be relieved her boyfriend isn't a murderer."

"Yeah, but it's over between them," Carla said. "She told me she can't trust him. He's a liar and a thief."

Bethany smiled wryly. "She has a point."

"Costa also left her a stipend in his will, to further her education in the future. I think she feels she owes it to him to really focus on studies."

"That's creepy. Like he knew he was going to die?"

Carla considered that a moment. "He probably *was* beginning to suspect that he might be in over his head with the duke's Port; what he thought was the duke's Port. But I think it was more because caring about Maria's future made him realize he'd better make a will." She explained the inheritance law to Bethany, then leaned toward the screen. "You want to hear another ironic thing in this case?"

At Bethany's nod, she said, "There's probably *three* forgeries. The one Paulo left in Pereira's cellar. The one given to Vitore that was supposed to be the real deal, but wasn't. And this third one that Costa was trying to sell back to Pereira. It's being tested now."

"Do they know who the forger is?"

"Oh, yeah. Vitore and O Lobo both gave the police his name. Some guy in Porto. He probably has the original bottle."

"What makes you say that?"

"The Porto police went to arrest him, and it seems he's closed shop and gone to Brazil."

That was the last crumb of information she'd been able to wangle out of Detective Fernandes before he said, "And now you know more than you need to know about something that is no longer your concern."

"Jeez, why Brazil?" Bethany asked.

Thinking of Torre's words, Carla said, "It's a place where people can disappear and not be found. Brazil is big. If you change your name, no one can find you." Senhora Gonzaga's sad confession of hoping to go to Brazil with Costa, posing as his wife, stirred a brief ripple of sympathy that quickly vanished. *She was going to kill you, kiddo! And she really did murder him.*

"So, I guess all's well that ends well," Bethany was saying.

"True," Carla murmured. "For some of us, anyway."

Chapter Twenty-Nine – A Fine Alvarinho

It had been chilly all day, with only a brief reappearance of the sun's warmth, so Carla wore a shawl. They were at Felix Taberna again—this time indoors, enjoying the soft glow of wall sconces and flickering shadows from the candle at their table. Duck rice, a house specialty, was followed by cheesecake and espresso. The past week might never have happened as she and Owen talked about the coming week-end in Ponte de Lima.

It's the oldest village in Portugal," he told her again with boyish enthusiasm. He must have memorized the entire Wikipedia summary. "It's named for the Roman bridge across the Lima River. That's what Ponte de Lima means, you know. The Bridge at the River Lima."

"I like the room you picked," Carla said, thinking of the website photos he'd shown her. One street away from the river, high on a slope with views from every room. The photographs showed an all-white attic interior with pitched ceilings, a white rug, white sofa, and lots of white cushions. "It looks like being inside a cloud."

Owen gave a pleased grin. "Tiago says they have good restaurants in Ponte de Lima, too."

"The perfect get-away. I'm so ready."

"Exactly." He reached over and cupped her chin. "You look beautiful tonight."

Later, holding hands, they walked along the cobbled Rua Dom Diego de Sousa, its street lamps bright under a gibbous moon. The courtyard outside the Sé Catedral was empty. The stone walls, rife with history, were somber and silent. The street soon merged into Rua do Souto. A few die-hard tourists straggled here and there, perhaps on their way to an after-dinner drink or simply on a late evening stroll.

Out of the blue, Owen said in a low voice, "Not to belabor things, babe, but . . .." His face was in shadow.

"But?"

"Please don't get involved in anything so dangerous again."

Carla gave a little laugh. "I don't expect to stumble across another dead body anytime soon." When he didn't answer, she leaned her head against his arm. Somehow, the "please" had sounded so bereft. "Sweetheart. Don't worry," she said. "I've learned my lesson. I'm just glad things are back to normal."

His answer was to press her hand, and then lightly rub her nails and cuticles, stirring a pleasurable skin-prickle along the back of her hand and up her arm.

They came to the Praça da República. Assorted tourists and locals clustered around Café Vianna's outside tables despite the cooling evening. Streamers from the water jets in the huge plaza fountain whished into the air and delicately splashed down.

"Feel like another glass of wine?" Owen asked.

They took a table close to the fountain. A slim waitress wearing a maroon apron hurried up and took their orders—two Alvarinhos. She glided away and returned shortly with their glasses and the bottle of white wine, pouring each of them a generous amount.

Owen raised his glass. "This is the kind of evening we'll always remember after we go home," he said, nodding toward the lights playing on the fountain streamers and then looking around at the tables filled with lively customers, all immersed in conversation.

"We will." Carla blew him a kiss. They clinked glasses, and she took a sip, enjoying the light tartness, feeling thrilled all over again to be in Portugal. It was nearly eleven, but voices rose and fell, laughter spraying into the air like the fountain's arcs of water. Figures swayed, hands lifted and dipped expressively.

"Braga never sleeps, does it?" she murmured.

Her glance came to rest on the table behind Owen, where an older man sat alone, twirling a glass of red wine. *He looks so solitary,* she thought, taking in his gray, bushy eyebrows, his trim mustache and grizzled beard. His bearing was tidy and dignified. He wore a flat cap and a jacket with that special cut that said "European."

All alone, with so much festivity around him. How sad!

But he'd only been waiting, it seemed. A similarly-dressed man—this one thin, with a long face—joined him, sitting poised on the edge of his chair. The soft *sh-sh* of Portuguese drifted to Carla. Was it her imagination? Or was there was something shifty about their hunched postures, their cautious glances?

She lowered her eyes, so as not to be caught staring.

"After the grand opening in September, we should go to Lisbon," Owen said. "Take a couple of weeks for pure vacation before going home. In September, it should still be warm, especially farther south."

"I'd like that," Carla agreed. "Maybe we can hear some Fado." Natália had said Lisboa was the birthplace of Fado.

Her glance wandered back to the table behind him, just in time to see—so subtly it could almost be her imagination—the first man nod and the newcomer rise. Carla watched the latter weave around tables, disappearing into darkness beyond the corner at the end of the arcade.

Hmm.

"And then maybe include a few nights in a fishing village." Owen said.

Carla tore her attention from the older man who sat regarding his glass.

"There's so much to see in Portugal," she told Owen. Despite her best intention, she darted another look at the table behind him.

The man was gone. *Just like that!* Only his half-empty wineglass remained.

"What?" Owen asked, his dimples faintly visible, as he waited for whatever she was going to say.

"I was just thinking . . .." *Mind your own business, kiddo!* She tilted her head to one side and smiled at her husband, then took a sip of wine and slowly swallowed it. "I really like a fine Alvarinho, don't you?"

Acknowledgements

First and foremost I would like to thank Belanger Books for their continued support. I would also like to thank the Storytellers Writing Group, trusted beta readers: Skeeter, Nancy, Randall, Jennie, Rosi, your suggestions always strengthen the work. Thanks also, Kathy Asay and Michele Drier, fellow writers in the Sacramento chapter of Sisters in Crime, for reading early drafts, and Joana Prata in Braga, for reading a later draft and giving important feedback.

Friends in Galicia (Melanie & Craig Briggs, Terri & David Anderson, John & Ida Blackbeard) told me charming things about Braga which inspired my first visit. Manuel Calda Castro shared tons of pictures with me, as did Trevor Pope in Texas after a vacation to Portugal.

Others provided much needed information for writing this book. My deepest gratitude to:

For information regarding the Interior Design business and Hoteliers, Pat Emery, at Ambiance Design Services in Los Angeles, Jennifer Jones at Niche Design Interiors and Claudia Justel at Adeeni Design Galerie (both in San Francisco), and Leo Chandler, General Manager, La Rivage Hotel, Westin Sacramento

An article by travel writer Stuart Forster, followed by a Skype Conference, put me in touch with Rui Prata, then director of Museu Imagem in Braga. Prata filled us in on Braga history, toured the city with us after hours, and has become a valued friend, as has his daughter, Joana. Many people in Braga were generous with information and time and have become friends. At Posto de Turismo, Cristina (Ana) and Marcia answered endless questions and provided information in emails; Carla Pereira has made us part of her Portuguese family, and let one of my characters work in her uncle's store, Casa Stop. Marisa Da Luz, fadista extraordinaire, invited us to fado events. Inês Barbosa introduced us to the music of fado, as well as giving historical background on various parts of the city. Helena Veloso, co-owner of Centésima Página (one of the most unique book stores I've ever seen) has also been supportive. A big thanks to all of you.

For information about legal processes and proceedings in Portugal, I am grateful to Commander Jose Antonio Cardoso Barbosa, in Braga (who is nothing like the chilly Detective Fernandes in the book). The commander kindly met with us many times to share information he thought would be helpful. Thanks also go to Jairo Ivan Domingos Campos, Comissário in Porto, who kindly answered follow-up questions via email. Clara Silva da Costa, Advogada answered my questions about how wills work in Portugal.

John R. Modica, at Direct Auction Galleries in Chicago, and Peter O'Grady, at O'Gallerie Auctions in Portland, OR, answered questions I had about how auctions worked, and Anibal Pinto de Faria at P55 Art and Auctions in Porto, and Lidia Aguilar in Braga answered more specific questions about how they operate in Porto and Braga.

Much appreciation goes to Stefan Sällberg, Vintage Port, who provided information on Port history, bottling, labeling, and fraud issues, and to Louisa Fry, Marketing and Communication, Instituto dos Vinhos do Douro e Porto, for information specifically on wine fraud. Special thanks to Miguel Potes at Symington for information about vintage and antique Ports and for his permission to use the 1863 vintage Port from Quinto do Vezuvio in my book.

About the Author

Elizabeth Varadan is a former elementary teacher who has always loved music, art, and other cultures. She and her husband live in Sacramento, California, but travel frequently to Spain and Portugal. Her children's fiction has appeared in *Story Friends*, *Ladybug*, and *Skipping Stones Magazine*, as well as in the 2016 anthology, *Beyond Watson* (Belanger Books). Her middle-grade mystery featuring Sherlock Holmes, *Imogene and the Case of the Missing Pearls* (MX Publishing), was published in 2015. Her picture book, *Dragonella*, was published by Belanger Books in 2017 (English edition) and in 2018 (Spanish edition). Her story collection, Carnival of the Animals, was published in 2018, also by Belanger Books.

You can visit her at her blogs:

http://elizabethvaradansfourthwish.blogspot.com

http://victorianscribbles.blogsspot.com

or at her author page at Amazon:

https://www.amazon.com/Elizabeth-Varadan/e/B003VOTCFG

Belanger Books

Made in the USA
Monee, IL
26 January 2020